U0025442

燈塔行

原著 Virginia Woolf

改寫 Elspeth Rawstron

譯者 安卡斯

To the Lighthouse

ABOUT THIS BOOK

For the Student

 Listen to the story and do some activities on your Audio CD.

 Talk about the story.

For the Teacher

Go to our Readers Resource site for information on using readers and downloadable Resource Sheets, photocopiable Worksheets, and Tapescripts. www.helblingreaders.com

You can download the Answer Key from the official site of Cosmos Publisher: www.icosmos.com.tw

For lots of great ideas on using Graded Readers consult Reading Matters, the Teacher's Guide to using Helbling Readers.

Structures

Modal verb would	Non-defining relative clauses
I'd love to . . .	Present perfect continuous
Future continuous	Used to / would
Present perfect future	Used to / used to doing
Reported speech / verbs / questions	Second conditional
Past perfect	Expressing wishes and regrets
Defining relative clauses	

Structures from other levels are also included.

CONTENTS

Virginia Woolf was born on 25th January 1882 in London. Her parents were wealthy[1] and their home was comfortable. Virginia grew up surrounded by books and intelligent[2] conversation.

Virginia Woolf had a tragic life. Many of the people closest to her died prematurely[3] and she suffered a number of nervous breakdowns[4] throughout her life. After her father's death in 1904, Virginia moved to the Bloomsbury area of London. Here, with her brother and friends, she helped form the Bloomsbury Group. The group was an intellectual[5] circle[6] of writers and artists who greatly influenced[7] cultural attitudes[8] in Britain in the early 20th century.

In 1912, Virginia married Leonard Woolf. He was the stable[9] presence that Virginia needed.

Virginia Woolf is acknowledged as one of the greatest innovators[10] in the English language and is a leading writer of the Modernist movement. She used a literary[11] device[12] called "stream of consciousness"[13] to give voice to her characters'[14] thoughts.

She wrote nine novels, two biographies, a volume of short stories, five volumes of collected essays[15] and reviews[16], and a volume of selections from her diary. Her most famous novels are: *Mrs. Dalloway*, *To the Lighthouse* and *A Room of One's Own*.

In March 1941, Virginia drowned[17] herself in a river near her East Sussex home. In a letter to her husband she said that she felt she was going insane[18] and she did not want to spoil his life, too.

---

1 wealthy [ˈwɛlθɪ] (a.) 富有的
2 intelligent [ɪnˈtɛlədʒənt] (a.) 有才智的
3 prematurely [ˌprɪməˈtjʊrlɪ] (adv.) 過早地
4 nervous breakdown 精神崩潰
5 intellectual [ˌɪntlˈɛktʃʊəl] (a.) 知識分子的
6 circle [ˈsɝkl] (n.) 圈子
7 influence [ˈɪnflʊəns] (v.) 影響
8 attitude [ˈætətjud] (n.) 觀點；態度
9 stable [ˈstebl] (a.) 穩重的
10 innovator [ˈɪnəˌvetɚ] (n.) 革新者
11 literary [ˈlɪtəˌrɛrɪ] (a.) 文學的
12 device [dɪˈvaɪs] (n.) 手法
13 stream of consciousness 意識流
14 character [ˈkærɪktɚ] (n.) 角色
15 essay [ˈɛse] (n.) 散文
16 review [rɪˈvju] (n.) 評論
17 drown [draʊn] (v.) 淹死
18 insane [ɪnˈsen] (a.) 精神錯亂的

To the Lighthouse is Virginia Woolf's most autobiographical[1] novel. When her sister Vanessa Bell, a painter like Lily Briscoe, read *To the Lighthouse*, she felt that their parents lived again in its pages. Her husband, Leonard, said it was a masterpiece[2].

Virginia and her family spent every summer until she was thirteen at a summer house in St Ives in Cornwall. Her mother, like Mrs Ramsay in the novel, invited friends from London to stay and the house was always full of guests. And as dusk[3] fell, they watched the beam[4] from Godrevy Lighthouse. After her mother's death in 1895, her father, like Mr Ramsay, didn't want to go there any more.

Godrevy Lighthouse in St. Ives Bay, Cornwall

The novel develops a series of thoughts rather than a plot, centering on themes like women's role in society, death and change. Virginia Woolf grew up in a time when women were wives and mothers and male domination[5] in society was the norm[6].

She rejected[7] these attitudes and her novel punishes women who accept the roles of wife and mother. Marriages end in tragedy or boredom[8], childbearing[9] ends in death and only independent single women survive[10].

Because she was deeply affected[11] by deaths in her family, Virginia Woolf wanted the characters in her novel to defeat[12] death. Mrs Ramsay wants to be remembered after her death, Mr Ramsay wants people to read his books after his death and Lily Briscoe would like to see her paintings hung for posterity[13]. All the characters are seeking a sense of permanence[14], and perhaps the author was, too.

1 autobiographical [ˌɔtəˌbaɪəˈgræfɪkl̩] (a.) 自傳性的
2 masterpiece [ˈmæstɚˌpis] (n.) 傑作
3 dusk [dʌsk] (n.) 黃昏
4 beam [bim] (n.) 光束
5 domination [ˌdɑməˈneʃən] (n.) 主宰
6 norm [nɔrm] (n.) 規範
7 reject [rɪˈdʒɛkt] (v.) 拒絕
8 boredom [ˈbɔrdəm] (n.) 無聊；厭倦
9 childbearing [ˈtʃaɪldˌbɛrɪŋ] (n.) 分娩
10 survive [səˈvaɪv] (v.) 活下來
11 affect [əˈfɛkt] (v.) 影響
12 defeat [dɪˈfit] (v.) 戰勝
13 posterity [pɑsˈtɛrətɪ] (n.) 後世
14 permanence [ˈpɝmənəns] (n.) 永恆

1 The lighthouse is a symbol of many things in the novel. Circle three words below that best describe the lighthouse for you.

calm
comforting
dangerous
distant
lonely
mysterious
peaceful
permanent
protective
tall

2 Complete the sentence with one of the words above. Check your answer after you have read the book.

"She looked at the long steady stroke of the Lighthouse, the last of the three, which was her stroke. She felt _____ again."

3 Have you ever been to a lighthouse or seen a lighthouse? Describe your experience. Then tell the class.

4 Sometimes places hold special memories. The lighthouse is special to the characters in the novel. Is there a building that is special to you? It may be a house, a castle or a museum. Write a paragraph about it.

When did you visit it?
Who did you go with?
Why is it special?

5 Find these lines from *The Charge of the Light Brigade* in the novel. Decide on their meaning in the context of the novel.

The Charge of the Light Brigade is a poem by Alfred Tennyson about an episode of the Crimean War. On 25th October 1854 near Balaclava, because of an error, either from the high command or from bad communication, more than one hundred men of the British cavalry were led to their death against Russian forces down a narrow valley.

A
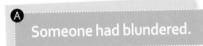
Someone had blundered.

Who had "blundered" (made a mistake)?
☐ Mr Ramsay, because he didn't pursue his studies to the full.
☐ Mrs Ramsay, because she only liked domestic life.

B
Attacked by gunshot and shell, bravely we rode and well, through the valley of Death.

What does this picture of bravery under gunshot and shell bring to mind?
☐ Facing life and daily events in a heroic way.
☐ Standing still and watching everyday life go by.

C Who sees life as a series of heroic events?

- ☐ Mrs Ramsay
- ☐ Mr Ramsay
- ☐ Lily Briscoe
- ☐ William Bankes

6 Listen to Mrs Ramsay and match the names of the characters to the pictures.

1. Lily Briscoe
2. Charles Tansley
3. Mr Ramsay
4. Mr Carmichael

7 Complete the sentences with the adjectives from the listening activity.

talented	bad-tempered
scruffy	dull
independent	disagreeable

a. I didn't enjoy the dinner. The conversation was

_____.

b. James is a good artist. He's very _____.

c. Andrew told Prue that no one would ever want to marry her. Brothers sometimes say some very _____ things.

d. Mr Ramsay was angry and he shouted at the gardener. He could be very _____.

e. Cam likes to do things by herself. She is a very _____ child.

f. He looked very _____ last night. His jacket had a hole in the sleeve and his trousers hadn't been ironed.

8 Complete the sentences from the novel with the words below. Look at the pages and check.

uncharming
confided
stupidity
admired
failure

a) The _____ of women's minds annoyed him. (Page 40)

b) He wanted sympathy. "He was a _____," he said. (Page 43)

c) She _____ the greatness of man's intellect. (Page 21)

d) "He was the most _____ man she had ever met," Lily Briscoe thought. Then why did she mind what he said? "Women can't write; women can't paint." (Page 69)

e) Generally, people liked her. They _____ in her. (Page 46)

9 Predict the answers to the questions below.

a Look at the picture of the house on page 79.
Why do the characters stop going to the house?

1 They have to sell the house for financial reasons.

2 Somebody dies in the family.

3 There is a ghost in the house.

b Look at the picture of Lily Briscoe on page 95.
What has happened?

1 She has become a famous artist.

2 She has found some meaning to life.

3 She has bought the house.

I. THE WINDOW

"Yes, of course, if it's fine tomorrow," said Mrs Ramsay. "But you'll have to get up very early," she added.

These words made her six-year-old son very happy. It was settled[1]. The expedition[2] was going to take place[3]. He had looked forward to[4] this adventure for years and years. And after a night's darkness and a day's sail, it was finally going to happen.

James Ramsay, sitting on the floor, cutting out pictures from a catalogue[5], was very happy. His mother watched him cut neatly[6] round the refrigerator. "He looks very serious," she thought. "I can imagine him as a judge[7], dressed in a red robe[8] with white fur[9], or helping the country through a crisis[10]."

"But, it won't be fine," said James's father, as he stopped in front of the drawing room[11] window.

---

1 settle [ˈsɛtl] (v.) 確定下來
2 expedition [ˌɛkspɪˈdɪʃən] (n.) 遠征；探險
3 take place 發生
4 look forward to 期待（後接名詞或動名詞）
5 catalogue [ˈkætəlɔg] (n.) 商品的型錄
6 neatly [ˈnitlɪ] (a.) 整潔的
7 judge [dʒʌdʒ] (n.) 法官
8 robe [rob] (n.) 長袍
9 fur [fɝ] (n.) 毛皮
10 crisis [ˈkraɪsɪs] (n.) 危機
11 drawing room 起居室

At that moment, James wanted to kill his father. Mr Ramsay always provoked[1] strong emotions[2] in his children. He stood there, thin as a knife. And he was smiling with the pleasure of disappointing[3] his son and ridiculing[4] his wife, who was ten thousand times better than him (James thought).

Mr Ramsay was always right, and he knew it. What he said was true. It was always true. He never changed a disagreeable[5] word to make somebody happy, least of all his own children.

"They should be aware[6] from childhood that life is difficult," he thought.

"But it may be fine," said Mrs Ramsay, as she was knitting[7] the brown sock.

If she managed to finish the sock and if they did go to the Lighthouse, she wanted to give it to the Lighthouse keeper for his little boy. She also wanted to give him some old magazines and some tobacco[8]. She would take all the things lying about the house that were not really wanted. She wanted to give those poor people something to amuse[9] them. They must be bored to death[10] sitting all day with nothing to do except polish[11] the lamp.

"How would you like to be shut up for a month in stormy weather, on a rock the size of a tennis court[12]? How would you like to see nobody? How would you like to see the same boring waves week after week? How would you like that?" she asked her daughters. "We must take them whatever comforts[13] we can."

---

1 provoke [prəˋvok] (v.) 挑釁；激怒
2 emotion [ɪˋmoʃən] (n.) 情緒
3 disappoint [ˌdɪsəˋpɔɪnt] (v.) 使失望
4 ridicule [ˋrɪdɪkjul] (n.) (v.) 揶揄
5 disagreeable [ˌdɪsəˋgriəb!] (a.) 惹人厭的

Alone

- Do you like being on your own or do you prefer being with other people?
- Imagine what it is like to be a lighthouse keeper. Share with a friend.

"The wind is due west[14]," said the atheist[15] Tansley.

A due west wind was the worst wind for landing at the Lighthouse.

Yes, he did say disagreeable things, Mrs Ramsay thought. Now James was even more disappointed. But she did not let the children laugh at Tansley. "The little atheist," the children called him. Rose made fun of him. Prue made fun of him. Andrew, Jasper and Roger made fun of him.

Mrs Ramsay hated incivility[16] to her guests, especially to young men. She had invited lots of poor but very talented[17] young men to stay with them on holiday on the Isle of Skye. Indeed, she had the whole of the male sex under her protection; for their chivalry[18] and bravery, for the fact that they made treaties[19], ruled India and controlled finance[20].

---

6 aware [əˈwɛr] (a.) 察覺的
7 knit [nɪt] (v.) 編織
8 tobacco [təˈbæko] (n.) 菸草
9 amuse [əˈmjuz] (v.) 娛樂；消遣
10 be bored to death 無聊至極
11 polish [ˈpolɪʃ] (v.) 擦亮
12 tennis court 網球場
13 comfort [ˈkʌmfət] (v.) 使安慰

14 due west 正西風
15 atheist [ˈeθɪɪst] (n.) 無神論者
16 incivility [ˌɪnsəˈvɪlətɪ] (n.) 無禮
17 talented [ˈtæləntɪd] (a.) 有才華的
18 chivalry [ˈʃɪvlrɪ] (n.) 對婦女的殷勤體貼
19 treaty [ˈtritɪ] (n.) 條約
20 finance [faɪˈnæns] (n.) 財政金融

When she looked in the mirror and saw her gray hair, at fifty, she thought: "I could have managed things better — my husband, money, his books. But I never regret my decision to get married."

She was a formidable[1] woman, and it was only in silence that her daughters, Prue, Nancy and Rose, could think of a different life from their mother's — a life in Paris, perhaps. A wilder life where they didn't always have to take care of a man. They all silently questioned[2] their mother's values of duty[3] and marriage, a silent questioning of dutifulness[4] and of ringed fingers[5] and beauty.

"You can't go to the Lighthouse tomorrow," said Charles Tansley, clapping his hands together as he stood at the window with her husband. Surely, he had said enough.

"I wish they would both leave James and me alone," she thought as she looked at him. "He's such a miserable[6] man, the children say. He can't play cricket[7]. He shuffles[8]. He's sarcastic[9]. What he likes best is walking up and down with Mr Ramsay, and saying who's won this, who's won that, who's the best at Latin[10] verses[11], who's the cleverest man in Balliol[12]. That's what they talk about."

---

1 formidable [ˈfɔrmɪdəbl] (a.) 難對付的
2 question [ˈkwɛstʃən] (v.) 懷疑
3 duty [ˈdjutɪ] (n.) 義務
4 dutifulness [ˈdjutɪfəlnɪs] (n.) 克盡本分
5 ringed fingers 婚姻
6 miserable [ˈmɪzərəbl] (a.) 悲哀的
7 cricket [ˈkrɪkɪt] (n.) 板球
8 shuffle [ˈʃʌfl] (v.) 拖著腳走路
9 sarcastic [sɑrˈkæstɪk] (a.) 好挖苦人的
10 Latin [ˈlætɪn] (a.) 拉丁語的
11 verse [vɜs] (n.) 詩；韻文
12 Balliol 牛津大學的貝列爾學院

Mrs Ramsay was standing by the drawing room window now. She was thinking of the problem of rich and poor, and the things she saw with her own eyes both here and in London, when she visited this widow[13], or that struggling[14] wife. With a notebook and pencil, she wrote down wages[15] and spendings[16], employment[17] and unemployment[18]. It was an unsolvable[19] problem.

Mr Tansley had followed her into the drawing room. He was standing by the table. They had all gone — the children, Minta Doyle and Paul Rayley, Augustus Carmichael and her husband.

So she turned with a sigh and said, "Would you like to come with me, Mr Tansley? I have to do a dull[20] errand[21] in the town. I've got a letter or two to write. I'll be ten minutes. I'll put on my hat."

And, with her basket and her parasol[22], there she was again, ten minutes later, ready.

She stopped for a moment to ask Mr Carmichael if he wanted anything. The man was dozing[23] with his yellow cat's eyes half open. And like a cat's eyes they reflected the branches[24] moving or the clouds passing but they didn't show any of his thoughts or emotions.

---

13 widow ['wɪdo] (n.) 寡婦
14 struggling ['strʌglɪŋ] (a.) 為生活掙扎的
15 wage [wedʒ] (n.) 薪水
16 spending ['spɛndɪŋ] (n.) 開銷
17 employment [ɪm'plɔɪmənt] (n.) 受雇
18 unemployment [ˌʌnɪm'plɔɪmənt] (n.) 失業
19 unsolvable [ʌn'sɑlvəbḷ] (a.) 無法解決的
20 dull [dʌl] (a.) 乏味的
21 errand ['ɛrənd] (n.) 差事
22 parasol ['pærəˌsɔl] (n.) 陽傘
23 doze [doz] (v.) 打瞌睡
24 branch [bræntʃ] (n.) 樹枝

"We're making the great expedition," she said, laughing. "We're going to the town. Stamps, writing paper, tobacco?" she suggested.

But no, he didn't want anything.

"He could have been a great philosopher[1]," said Mrs Ramsay, as they went down the road to the fishing village. "But he made the wrong marriage."

Holding up her black parasol, she told the story; an affair[2] at Oxford with a girl; an early marriage; poverty; going to India; translating[3] a little poetry[4] "very beautifully, I believe," and then lying, as they saw him, on the lawn.

It flattered[5] Charles Tansley that Mrs Ramsay should tell him this. He felt better. She admired the greatness of man's intellect[6] and believed in the subjection[7] of all wives to their husband's work. She didn't blame[8] the girl, and the marriage had been quite happy, she believed.

Mrs Ramsay made Mr Tansley feel better about himself. And if they took a cab[9], he would like to pay the fare[10]. As for her little bag, could he carry that?

No, she said. *She* always carried *that* herself. She did too. Yes, he felt that in her. He felt many things, and something in particular that excited him and disturbed him at the same time.

---

1 philosopher [fə'lɑsəfə] (n.) 哲學家
2 affair [ə'fɛr] (n.) 戀愛事件
3 translate [træns'let] (v.) 翻譯
4 little poetry 小品詩
5 flatter ['flætə] (v.) 奉承；使高興
6 intellect ['ɪntl,ɛkt] (n.) 才智
7 subjection [səb'dʒɛkʃən] (n.) 屈從
8 blame [blem] (v.) 指責；歸咎於
9 cab [kæb] (n.) 出租馬車
10 fare [fɛr] (n.) 車資

He would like her to see him in cap and gown[1], walking in a procession[2]. A professorship[3] — but what was she looking at? She was looking at a man putting up a poster[4]. Each movement of the brush showed more legs, hoops[5], horses, in bright reds and blues, until half the wall was covered with the advertisement[6] of a circus.

"A hundred horsemen, twenty performing[7] seals, lions, tigers . . . will visit this town," she read. "Let's all go!" she cried with childlike happiness.

"Let's go," he said, repeating her words, with a self-consciousness[8] that upset[9] her.

He could not say it right. He could not feel it right. But why not? she wondered. What was wrong with him then? She liked him, at that moment.

"Did no one take you to the circus when you were children?" she asked.

"Never," he answered.

He was from a large family, nine brothers and sisters, and his father was a working man.

"My father is a chemist[10], Mrs Ramsay. He's got a shop. I've paid my own way since I was thirteen."

Often he didn't have a coat in winter. He smoked the cheapest tobacco. He worked hard.

---

1 cap and gown 大學教授所穿的衣服
2 procession [prəˈsɛʃən] (n.) 行列
3 professorship [prəˈfɛsəˌʃɪp] (n.) 教授的職位
4 poster [ˈpostɚ] (n.) 海報
5 hoop [hup] (n.) 鐵環
6 advertisement [ˌædvɚˈtaɪzmənt] (n.) 廣告
7 performing [pɚˈfɔrmɪŋ] (a.) 會表演的
8 self-consciousness [ˈsɛlfˈkʌnʃənsnɪs] (n.) 自我意識
9 upset [ʌpˈsɛt] (v.) 使不適
10 chemist [ˈkɛmɪst] (n.) 藥師

To the Lighthouse

They walked on. Mrs Ramsay listened but did not quite understand the meaning, only some words: dissertation[1], fellowship[2], readership[3], lectureship[4].

She said to herself: "I won't let the children laugh at him any more, poor little man."

They had reached the town now and were in the main street. He went on talking, about teaching, and working men, and lectures[5] and he was about to tell her something when they walked out onto the quay[6].

The whole bay spread before them and Mrs Ramsay could not help exclaiming[7], "Oh, how beautiful!"

The great plateful[8] of blue water was before her; the Lighthouse, tall and distant in the middle; and on the right, as far as the eye could see, the green sand dunes[9] with the wild grasses on them.

"That's the view that my husband loves," she said, stopping.

Mr Tansley was now under the influence of an extraordinary[10] emotion. It had begun in the garden when he had wanted to take her bag, and it had increased in the town when he had wanted to tell her everything about himself. It was very strange.

---

1 dissertation [ˌdɪsəˈteʃən] (n.) 博士學位論文
2 fellowship [ˈfɛloˌʃɪp] (n.) 大學的研究員職位
3 readership [ˈridəˌʃɪp] (n.) 高級講師的職位
4 lectureship [ˈlɛktʃəˌʃɪp] (n.) 大學講師的職位
5 lecture [ˈlɛktʃə] (n.) 授課
6 quay [ki] (n.) 碼頭

7 exclaim [ɪksˈklem] (v.) 呼喊
8 plateful [ˈpletˌful] (n.)
　（一）滿盤
9 dune [djun] (n.) 沙丘
10 extraordinary
　[ɪkˈstrɔrdn̩ˌɛrɪ] (a.) 異常的

There he stood in the living room of the little house where she had taken him. He waited for her, while she went upstairs to see a woman. He heard her voice. He waited impatiently[1]. He looked forward to the walk home. He wanted to carry her bag.

Then he heard her come out, shut a door and say, "You must keep the windows open and the doors shut. Ask at the house for anything you want."

Then suddenly, when she walked into the room, he realized[2] that she was the most beautiful person he had ever seen.

With stars in her eyes and the wind in her hair—what nonsense[3] was he thinking? She was fifty at least. She had eight children. Stepping through fields of flowers with the stars in her eyes and the wind in her hair. He took her bag.

"Goodbye, Elsie," she said, and they walked up the street.

A man digging[4] in a drain[5] stopped digging and looked at her. And for the first time in his life, Charles Tansley felt very proud. He was walking with a beautiful woman. He was holding her bag.

---

1 impatiently [ɪmˈpeʃəntlɪ]
  (adv.) 沒耐性地
2 realize [ˈrɪəˌlaɪz] (v.) 領悟到
3 nonsense [ˈnɑnsɛns] (n.) 蠢話
4 dig [dɪg] (v.) 挖
5 drain [dren] (n.) 排水道

"You can't go to the Lighthouse, James," said Mr Tansley.

"Nasty[6] little man," thought Mrs Ramsay. "Why does he keep saying that?"

"Perhaps we'll wake up and find the sun shining and the birds singing," she said kindly, smoothing[7] James's hair.

James really wanted to go to the Lighthouse.

She couldn't hear voices any more. They had stopped talking. She listened, and then heard something rhythmical[8], half said, half chanted[9], beginning in the garden. Suddenly there was a loud cry:

"Stormed[10] at with shot and shell[11]!"[12]

She turned nervously to see if anyone had heard her husband. Only Lily Briscoe, she was glad to find; and that did not matter. But the sight of the girl standing on the edge of the lawn painting reminded her that she was supposed to keep her head in the same position[13] for Lily's picture. Lily's picture! Mrs Ramsay smiled.

"With her little Chinese eyes and pale face, she'll never marry," she thought.

---

6 nasty ['næstɪ] (a.) 討人厭的
7 smooth [smuð] (v.) 使平整
8 rhythmical ['rɪðmɪk!] (n.) 有節奏的
9 chant [tʃænt] (v.) 唱；吟誦
10 storm [stɔrm] (v.) 猛攻
11 shot and shell 槍彈和砲彈

12 出自英國詩人丁尼生（Alfred Tennyson）的詩〈The Charge Of The Light Brigade〉，內容在紀念英國輕騎兵在克里米亞戰爭期間的英勇事蹟。當時英國指揮官下錯指令，命令六百餘名輕騎兵向 Balaclava 的俄國陣營衝鋒，結果變成了慘烈的自殺式進攻。
13 position [pə'zɪʃən] (n.) 姿勢

🎧 You could not take her painting very seriously. She was an independent[1] little woman, and Mrs Ramsay liked her because of this. So, remembering her promise, she bent her head.

Mr Ramsay almost knocked Lily's easel[2] over[3], running towards her with his hands waving, shouting out:

"Bravely we rode and well[4]."

Thankfully, he turned, and rode off, to die gloriously[5], at Balaclava, Lily supposed.

He was frightening and ridiculous at the same time. But as long as he was waving and shouting, she was safe.

"He won't stand and look at my picture," she thought, relieved[6]. "I don't want anyone to look at my picture."

Imagine

- Imagine the scene. What is happening? Tick the correct sentence from each pair. Then close your eyes and picture the scene.

☐ Mrs Ramsay and Lily are in the house.
☐ Mrs Ramsay and Lily are in the garden.

☐ Lily is painting Mrs Ramsay's portrait[7].
☐ Lily is talking to Mrs Ramsay.

☐ Mr Ramsay runs across the lawn shouting.
☐ Mr Ramsay stops and looks at the painting.

But now someone else was walking towards her. She could tell[8] from the footsteps that it was William Bankes. But she did not turn her picture over on the grass. She would have turned it over if it had been anybody else.

They were both staying in the village, and walking in and out, they had talked about the soup, about the children, about one thing and another, which made them friends. Now when he stood beside her, she just stood there. (He was old enough to be her father, a botanist[9], a widower[10], smelling of soap, very tidy[11] and clean.)

Staying in the same house with her, he had noticed how organized[12] she was. She got up before breakfast and went to paint. She was poor, and not as attractive as Miss Doyle. However, she was sensible[13], which made her, in his eyes, superior[14] to Miss Doyle. Now, for instance, when Ramsay came, shouting, and waving his arms, Miss Briscoe understood.

"Someone had blundered[15]."

---

1 independent [ˌɪndɪˈpɛndənt] (a.) 獨立的
2 easel [ˈizl̩] (n.) 畫架
3 knock over 撞倒
4 well [wɛl] (v.) 湧出；湧上
5 gloriously [ˈglorɪəslɪ] (adv.) 輝煌地
6 relieve [rɪˈliv] (v.) 使放心
7 portrait [ˈportret] (n.) 肖像
8 tell [tɛl] (v.) 分辨
9 botanist [ˈbɑtənɪst] (n.) 植物學家
10 widower [ˈwɪdɚ] (n.) 鰥夫
11 tidy [ˈtaɪdɪ] (a.) 整潔的
12 organized [ˈɔrgənˌaɪzd] (a.) 有組織的
13 sensible [ˈsɛnsəbl̩] (a.) 靈敏的
14 superior [səˈpɪrɪɚ] (a.) 較好的
15 blunder [ˈblʌndɚ] (v.) 鑄錯

🎧 Mr Ramsay glared[1] at them. That made them both uncomfortable. Together they had seen a thing they were not meant to see.

Quickly, Mr Bankes said something about it being cold. He suggested going for a walk. She agreed. But it was difficult to leave her picture.

She loved painting, but when she began to paint, she felt inadequate[2]. She laid[3] her brushes[4] neatly in the box, and said to William Bankes, "Yes, it's cold now."

It was the middle of September after all, and past six in the evening.

They walked down the garden; past the tennis lawn, past the tall grass, to that gap[5] in the thick hedge, guarded by red-hot pokers[6]. Between them, the blue waters of the bay looked bluer than ever.

They came there every evening. They both smiled, standing there. They felt happy.

Looking at the sand dunes, William Bankes thought of Ramsay, thought of a road in Westmorland, thought of Ramsay walking along that road ahead of him. He thought their friendship had ended, there, on that road.

After that, Ramsay had married. After that, their friendship had changed. But he said he still admired and respected Ramsay.

---

1 glare [glɛr] (v.) 怒視
2 inadequate [ɪnˋædəkwɪt] (a.) 不能勝任的
3 lay [le] (v.) 置放（動態三態：lay; laid; laid）
4 brush [brʌʃ] (n.) 畫筆
5 gap [gæp] (n.) 空地
6 hedge [hɛdʒ] (n.) 樹籬
7 red-hot poker 劍葉蘭

He turned from the view. They started to walk up the drive[1] to the house. They saw Cam, Ramsay's youngest daughter. She was picking flowers. She was wild and fierce[2]. She would not "give a flower to the gentleman" as the nursemaid[3] told her to. No! no! no! she would not! She stamped[4] her feet. And Mr Bankes felt old and sad then.

The Ramsays were not rich. And they had eight children! How can anybody feed eight children on philosophy[5]? There was their education to pay for (true, Mrs Ramsay had some money of her own perhaps) and there were the clothes.

Values

- What is more important in your opinion? Number the boxes.
  - ☐ Having a happy marriage
  - ☐ Being successful in your job
  - ☐ Educating your children
  - ☐ Having friends

1 drive [draɪv] (n.) 車道
2 fierce [fɪrs] (a.) 兇巴巴的
3 nursemaid [ˋnɝsˏmed] (n.) 保姆
4 stamp [stæmp] (v.) 踩
5 philosophy [fəˋlɑsəfɪ] (n.) 哲學

They walked up the drive, and Lily Briscoe said "yes" and "no" to his comments. He talked about Ramsay. He felt sorry for him but he also envied[6] him.

The children gave Ramsay something — William Bankes acknowledged[7] that. He wished Cam had stuck[8] a flower in his coat or climbed over his shoulders, as she did over her father's.

But the children had also destroyed[9] something, his old friends thought. What did Lily Briscoe think? It was surprising that a man of his intellect depended on people's praise[10] as much as he did.

"Oh, but," said Lily, "think of his work!"

Whenever she "thought of his work" she always saw a large kitchen table. It was Andrew's fault.

"What are your father's books about?" she had asked him.

"Subject[11] and object[12] and the nature[13] of reality[14]," Andrew had said.

And when she said she didn't know what that meant.

"Think of a kitchen table when you're not there," Andrew had told her.

So now when she thought of Mr Ramsay's work, she always saw a kitchen table.

---

6 envy [ˈɛnvɪ] (v.) 羨慕
7 acknowledge [əkˈnɑlɪdʒ] (v.) 認可
8 stick [stɪk] (v.)〔口〕放置（動詞三態：stick; stuck; stuck）
9 destroy [dɪˈstrɔɪ] (v.) 毀壞
10 praise [prez] (n.) 稱讚
11 subject [ˈsʌbdʒɪkt] (n.) 主體
12 object [ˈɑbdʒɪkt] (n.) 客體
13 nature [ˈnetʃɚ] (n.) 本質
14 reality [riˈælətɪ] (n.) 實體；真實

William Bankes liked her for telling him to "think of his work." He had thought of it, often. Many times he had said, "Ramsay is one of those men who do their best work before they're forty."

He had made a definite[1] contribution[2] to philosophy in one little book when he was only twenty-five. What came after that was more or less repetition[3].

At that moment, Lily Briscoe felt a great respect for Mr Bankes. You are not vain[4]. You are better than Mr Ramsay. You are the best human being that I know. You don't have any children or a wife. You live for science. Praise is an insult[5] to you. You are a kind, generous, heroic[6] man!

But then, she remembered how he had brought a valet[7] all the way up to Scotland. He didn't like dogs on chairs. He talked for hours about salt in vegetables and bad English cooks. How then did you judge people? How did you decide that you liked them or disliked them?

Standing now, staring at the pear tree, she thought about the two men. Following her thoughts was like following a voice which speaks too quickly for your pencil to write it all down. And her voice was saying contradictory[8] things.

---

1 definite [ˈdɛfənɪt] (a.) 一定的
2 contribution [ˌkɑntrəˈbjuʃən] (n.) 貢獻
3 repetition [ˌrɛpɪˈtɪʃən] (n.) 重複
4 vain [ven] (a.) 自負的
5 insult [ˈɪnsʌlt] (n.) 羞辱
6 heroic [hɪˈroɪk] (a.) 英雄的
7 valet [ˈvælɪt] (n.) 貼身男僕
8 contradictory [ˌkɑntrəˈdɪktərɪ] (a.) 矛盾的
9 spoilt [spoɪlt] (a.) 被寵壞的
10 tyrant [ˈtaɪrənt] (n.) 專橫的人
11 address [əˈdrɛs] (v.) 對……說話
12 dynamic [daɪˈnæmɪk] (a.) 有活力的

Mr Ramsay is selfish and vain. He is spoilt[9]. He is a tyrant[10]. He tires Mrs Ramsay out. But he is what you (she addressed[11] Mr Bankes in her mind) are not. He is dynamic[12]. He knows nothing about trivial[13] things. He loves dogs and his children. He has eight. Mr Bankes has none.

    All of this danced up and down, in Lily's mind. A shot went off nearby, and there came, flying from its fragments[14], a frightened flock[15] of birds.

    "Jasper!" said Mr Bankes.

    They turned to watch the birds fly over the terrace[16]. Following the scatter[17] of swift[18]-flying birds in the sky, they stepped through the gap in the hedge and bumped into[19] Mr Ramsay, who shouted tragically[20] at them:

"Someone had blundered."

---

13 trivial [ˈtrɪvɪəl] (a.) 瑣細的
14 fragment [ˈfrægmənt] (n.) 碎片
15 flock [flɑk] (n.) 畜群
16 terrace [ˈtɛrəs] (n.) 露臺
17 scatter [ˈskætɚ] (n.) 散布
18 swift [swɪft] (a.) 迅速的
19 bump into 撞見
20 tragically [ˈtrædʒɪklɪ] (adv.) 悲劇性地

Mr Ramsay looked at Lily and Mr Bankes for a second, and he almost recognized[1] them. Then he turned away quickly.

Lily Briscoe and Mr Bankes looked nervously up into the sky, and watched the flock of birds, which Jasper had shot at with his gun. They were sitting on the tops of the trees.

"And even if it isn't fine tomorrow," said Mrs Ramsay, looking up at William Bankes and Lily Briscoe as they passed, "it will be another day. And now . . .," she said, thinking that Lily's charm was her Chinese eyes, in her pale face, but it would take a clever man to see it. "And now stand up, and let me measure[2] your leg. We might go to the Lighthouse, and I must see if the sock is long enough."

Smiling, for she had just had a brilliant[3] idea. William and Lily should marry. She took the sock and measured it against James's leg.

Then she looked up and saw the room, and the chairs, and thought they were very shabby[4]. But what's the point of buying good chairs? They'll get spoilt up here in the wet winter. But never mind! The rent was only two and a half pence[5]. The children loved it. It did her husband good to be three thousand, or if she must be accurate[6], three hundred miles from his libraries and his lectures; and there was room for visitors.

---

1 recognize [ˈrɛkəɡˌnaɪz] (v.) 理睬
2 measure [ˈmɛʒɚ] (v.) 測量
3 brilliant [ˈbrɪljənt] (a.) 很妙的
4 shabby [ˈʃæbɪ] (a.) 陳舊的
5 pence [pɛns] (n.) penny（便士）的複數（指錢的總數，與 pennies 有別，後者指個別的錢）
6 accurate [ˈækjərɪt] (a.) 準確的

"My dear, stand still[1]," she said to James. "Soon," she thought, "the house will become so shabby that something must be done."

If she could teach the children to wipe[2] their feet and not bring the beach[3] in with them — that would help. Things got shabbier and shabbier every summer. The mat[4] was fading[5]. The wallpaper was fading. You couldn't tell any more that those were roses on it.

She felt annoyed[6], and said sharply[7] to James, "Stand still."

The sock was too short by half an inch.

"It's too short," she said, "much too short."

Knitting her brown sock, Mrs Ramsay kissed her little boy on the forehead.

"Let's find another picture to cut out," she said.

"Someone had blundered."

Mrs Ramsay looked up.

"Someone had blundered."

---

1 still [stɪl] (adv.) 不動的
2 wipe [waɪp] (v.) 擦拭
3 beach [bitʃ] (n.) 海濱的砂石
4 mat [mæt] (n.) 腳踏墊
5 fade [fed] (v.) 褪色
6 annoyed [əˋnɔɪd] (a.) 心煩的
7 sharply [ˋʃɑrplɪ] (adv.) 嚴厲地

She looked up at her husband, who was now walking towards her. Something had happened; someone had made a mistake. But she didn't know what.

Mr Ramsay trembled[1]. Stormed at with gunshot and shell, bravely he rode and well, through the valley of death, straight into Lily Briscoe and William Bankes. He trembled.

Mrs Ramsay didn't speak to him. She realized from the familiar signs that he was very upset. She stroked[2] James's head. She transferred[3] to him what she felt for her husband, and she watched him color a white shirt in the catalogue yellow.

She'd be very happy if he became a great artist, she thought. And why shouldn't he?

Then, looking up, as her husband walked past again, she was relieved to see that he was calm now.

Domesticity[4] had won. He stopped at the window and bent to tickle[5] James's bare[6] leg. Hating his father, James brushed[7] his hand away.

"I'm trying to get these socks finished to send to the Lighthouse keeper's little boy tomorrow", said Mrs Ramsay.

"You can't go to the Lighthouse tomorrow," Mr Ramsay said bad-temperedly[8].

"How do you know?" she asked. "The wind often changes."

The stupidity of women's minds annoyed him. He stamped his foot on the stone step.

---

1 tremble [ˈtrɛmbl̩] (v.) 顫抖
2 stroke [strok] (v.) 用手輕撫
3 transfer [trænsˈfɝ] (v.) 轉移
4 domesticity [ˌdomɛsˈtɪsətɪ] (n.) 家居生活
5 tickle [ˈtɪkl̩] (v.) 搔癢
6 bare [bɛr] (a.) 裸露的
7 brush [brʌʃ] (v.) 拂去；推開
8 bad-temperedly [ˈbædˈtɛmpɚdlɪ] (adv.) 脾氣不好地

To the Lighthouse

"Damn you," he said.

But what had she said? Simply that it might be fine tomorrow. And so it might.

"Not with the temperature falling and the wind due west," he said.

"He has no consideration[9] for other people's feelings," she thought.

And she bent her head and said nothing. There was nothing to be said.

He stood by her in silence. Then, very humbly[10], he said, "I'll go and ask the coastguards[11] if you like."

"I'll take your word for it[12]," she said.

There was nobody she admired more. She was not good enough to tie his shoe laces, she felt.

Already ashamed of his bad temper, Mr Ramsay rather sheepishly[13] tickled his son's bare legs once more, and then, he walked out again into the evening air.

"Someone had blundered," he said again, walking up and down the terrace. But the tone of his voice had changed. "Someone had blundered," sounded ridiculous said like that. It had no conviction[14]. Mrs Ramsay could not help smiling. Soon, walking up and down, he hummed[15] it. Then he fell silent.

---

9 consideration [kənˌsɪdəˈreʃən] (n.) 體貼
10 humbly [ˈhʌmblɪ] (adv.) 謙遜地
11 coastguard [ˈkostˌgɑrd] (n.) 海巡員
12 take someone's word for it
　相信某人說的話

13 sheepishly [ˈʃipɪʃlɪ]
　(adv.) 羞怯地
14 conviction [kənˈvɪkʃən]
　(n.) 說服力
15 hum [hʌm] (v.) 哼曲子

He was safe. He stopped to light his pipe[1], looked once at his wife and son in the window, and the sight of them strengthened him and satisfied him. But his son hated him. He hated him for interrupting them.

They were reading a fairy tale[2]. He looked at the page. He wanted to make his father move away. He pointed his finger at a word. He wanted to get his mother's attention, which was with his father. But, no. Mr Ramsay didn't move away. He stood there, demanding[3] sympathy[4].

Mrs Ramsay prepared herself. He wanted sympathy.

"He was a failure[5]," he said.

She blew the words back at him. "Charles Tansley thinks you're the greatest metaphysician[6] of the time," she said.

But he needed more than that. He must have sympathy. He must know that he was needed, not only here, but all over the world.

Flashing[7] her knitting needles, confident[8], tall, she filled the room with warmth and light; told him to relax there, go in and out, enjoy himself.

She laughed. She knitted. Standing between her knees, James felt all her strength being drained[9] by his father's demands for sympathy.

"He was a failure," he repeated.

---

1 pipe [paɪp] (n.) 煙斗
2 fairy tale 童話故事
3 demand [dɪˋmænd] (v.) 需要
4 sympathy [ˋsɪmpəθɪ] (n.) 同情；慰問
5 failure [ˋfeljɚ] (n.) 失敗者
6 metaphysician [ˏmɛtəfəˋzɪʃən] (n.) 形而上學者
7 flash [flæʃ] (v.) 閃光
8 confident [ˋkɑnfədənt] (a.) 有信心的
9 drain [dren] (v.) 耗盡

Flashing her knitting needles, she assured[1] him, by her laugh, her calm, her competence[2]. If he put his faith[3] in her, nothing would hurt him. Filled with her words, he felt better. He looked at her with gratitude[4], and he said, "I'll go for a walk. I'll watch the children playing cricket." He went.

Immediately, Mrs Ramsay seemed to fold[5] herself together, one petal closed, then another. She was exhausted[6].

As she turned to the fairy tale again, Mrs Ramsay felt something disagreeable. She did not like, even for a second, to feel finer than her husband. She didn't like people seeing him coming to her like that. For then people said he depended on her. They must know that he was a much more important person than she was. What she gave the world, in comparison[7] with what he gave, was nothing.

But there was something else — she couldn't tell him the truth. She was afraid, for example, to tell him about the greenhouse[8] roof. "It'll cost fifty pounds to mend it." And then about his books — she was afraid that he might guess what she suspected[9], that his last book was not his best book (she understood that from William Bankes). All this diminished[10] the joy, the pure joy of their marriage.

A shadow was on the page; she looked up. It was Augustus Carmichael shuffling past in his yellow slippers.

"Are you going inside?" she called out.

---

1 assure [əˋʃur] (v.) 使放心
2 competence [ˋkɑmpətəns] (n.) 能力
3 faith [feθ] (n.) 信念
4 gratitude [ˋgrætəˏtjud] (n.) 感激之情
5 fold [fold] (v.) 抱住
6 exhausted [ɪgˋzɔstɪd] (a.) 精疲力竭的

7 comparison [kəmˋpærəsn̩] (n.) 比較
8 greenhouse [ˋgrinˏhaus] (n.) 溫室
9 suspect [səˋspɛkt] (v.) 懷疑
10 diminish [dəˋmɪnɪʃ] (v.) 減少
11 escape [əˋskep] (n.) 逃避
12 nasty [ˋnæstɪ] (a.) 脾氣不好的

He said nothing. She knew that the poor man was unhappy. He came to stay with them every year as an escape[11]; and yet every year she felt the same thing. He did not trust her. It was his wife's fault.

She remembered the time in the horrible little room in St John's Wood, when she had seen that nasty[12] woman send him out of the house. He was scruffy[13]; he dropped things on his coat; he was an old man with nothing in the world to do; and she sent him out of the house.

She said, in her nasty way, "Now, Mrs Ramsay and I want to have a little talk together," and Mrs Ramsay could see the many miseries of his life. Did he have enough money to buy tobacco? Did he have to ask his wife for it? Oh, she could not bear[14] to think of the humiliation[15] his wife made him suffer[16]. And now he always shrank[17] from her.

The guests

- Can you remember the names of Mrs Ramsay's guests?
  ① The little atheist: _____
  ② He could have been a great philosopher but made the wrong marriage: _____
  ③ A painter, an independent little woman:
     _____
  ④ An old friend of her husband, who still admired and respected him: _____

---

13 scruffy [ˈskrʌfɪ] (a.) 邋遢的
14 bear [bɛr] (v.) 忍受
15 humiliation [hju,mɪlɪˈeʃən] (n.) 羞辱
16 suffer [ˈsʌfɚ] (v.) 遭受

17 shrink [ʃrɪŋk] (v.) 退縮 (動
態三態 : shrink; shrank,
shrunk; shrunk, shrunken)

But what more could she do? She had given him a sunny room. The children were good to him. She went out of her way[1] to be friendly. Generally, people liked her. They confided[2] in her. She carried with her the torch[3] of her beauty. She carried it into every room that she entered.

She had better finish the story of *The Fisherman and his Wife* for her sensitive[4] son James (none of her children were as sensitive as he was).

Mrs Ramsay wished that her husband had not chosen that moment to stop. Why hadn't he gone to watch the children play cricket? But he did not speak; he looked; he nodded; and then he went into the garden.

He had read an article in *The Times* about the number of Americans who visit Shakespeare's house every year.

"If Shakespeare had never existed," he asked himself, "would the world be a different place today? Does the progress of civilization[5] depend on great men? Is the life of the average person better now than in the time of the Pharaohs[6]?" "Possibly not. Possibly the greatest good requires the existence[7] of a slave[8] class. The liftman[9] in the Tube[10] is a necessity. The world exists for the average person," he thought. "The arts are just a decoration placed on the top of human life. Shakespeare is not necessary to it."

---

1 go out of one's way 不怕麻煩
  地盡力去做
2 confide [kən'faɪd] (v.) 吐露祕密
3 torch [tɔrtʃ] (n.) 火炬
4 sensitive ['sɛnsətɪv] (a.) 敏感的

5 civilization [ˌsɪvḷə'zeʃən] (n.) 文明
6 pharaoh ['færo] (n.) 埃及法老王
7 existence [ɪg'zɪstəns] (n.) 存在
8 slave [slev] (n.) 奴隸
9 liftman ['lɪftmən] (n.) 電梯操作員

To the Lighthouse

He wasn't sure why he wanted to criticize[11] Shakespeare and praise the man who stands in the door of the lift. He had promised in six weeks" time to talk to the students of Cardiff University about Locke[12], Hume[13], Berkeley[14] and the causes[15] of the French Revolution[16]. And all this would be in his talk, he thought.

He was walking towards Lily and Mr Bankes. Then he stopped and stood looking in silence at the sea. Now he turned away again.

"Yes," Mr Bankes said, watching him go. "It's a shame that[17] Ramsay can't behave a little more like other people." (Because he liked Lily Briscoe, he could discuss Ramsay with her.)

"I like Mr Ramsay for thinking that, if his little finger hurts, the whole world must come to an end," she said. "What I dislike is his narrow-mindedness[18], his blindness," she said.

"He's a bit of[19] a hypocrite[20]?" Mr Bankes suggested, looking at Mr Ramsay's back.

He was thinking of his friendship, and of Cam refusing to give him a flower, and of all those boys and girls, and his own house, comfortable, but very quiet since his wife's death. Of course, he had his work . . . All the same, he wanted Lily to agree that Ramsay was "a bit of a hypocrite".

---

10 tube [tjub] (n.) 倫敦地鐵
11 criticize [ˋkrɪtəˏsaɪz] (v.) 批評；評論
12 John Locke 約翰・洛克，與大衛・休姆、喬治・貝克萊，同被列為英國經驗主義的代表人物
13 David Hume 大衛・休姆
14 George Berkeley 喬治・貝克萊
15 cause [kɔz] (n.) 起因
16 revolution [ˏrɛvəˋluʃən] (n.) 革命
17 it's a shame that . . . 只可惜……
18 narrow-mindedness [ˋnæroˋmaɪndɪdnɪs] (n.) 心胸狹窄
19 a bit of 有一點兒
20 hypocrite [ˋhɪpəkrɪt] (n.) 偽君子

Lily Briscoe went on putting away[1] her brushes, looking up, looking down. Looking up, there was Mr Ramsay — walking towards them.

"A bit of a hypocrite?" she repeated. "Oh, no — the most sincere of men, the truest (here he was), the best."

But, looking down, she thought, "he is self-centered[2]. He's tyrannical[3]. He's unjust."

Mr Bankes expected her to answer. And she was about to say something criticizing Mrs Ramsay, when she saw Mr Bankes gazing[4] adoringly[5] at Mrs Ramsay. This adoring look made Lily Briscoe forget what she was about to say. It was nothing important; something about Mrs Ramsay.

"Let him gaze; I'll look at my picture."

She wanted to cry. It was bad. It was very bad!

"I can't let anyone see it. It'll never be hung," she thought.

And there was Mr Tansley whispering in her ear, "Women can't paint; women can't write . . ."

Now, she remembered what she had wanted to say about Mrs Ramsay. Her arrogance[6] had annoyed her the other night. She was the loveliest of people; but also, she was domineering[7]. She was always insisting[8] that they all must marry. No matter how successful a woman was (Mrs Ramsay cared nothing for Lily's painting), she must marry.

"An unmarried woman has missed the best of life," she always said.

---

1 put away 收好
2 self-centered [ˌsɛlfˈsɛntəd] (a.) 自我的
3 tyrannical [taɪˈrænɪkl̩] (a.) 專橫的
4 gaze [gez] (v.) 凝視
5 adoringly [əˈdɔrɪŋlɪ] (adv.) 仰慕地
6 arrogance [ˈærəgəns] (n.) 自大

"Oh, but," Lily said, "There's my father; my home; and, (but she didn't dare[9] say this), my painting."

But all this seemed very little. She liked to be alone; she was not made for marriage. But Mrs Ramsay was certain that her dear Lily was a fool.

Lily turned to look at Mr Bankes. He had put on his glasses. He had stepped back. He had raised[10] his hand. He had slightly narrowed[11] his clear blue eyes.

Lily winced[12] like a dog that sees a hand raised to hit it. She wanted to pull her painting off the easel. But instead she prepared herself for the awful trial[13] of someone looking at her painting. And if someone must see it, Mr Bankes was better than the others.

Taking out a penknife[14], Mr Bankes tapped[15] the painting with the handle.

"What do you want to show by the purple shape, just there?" he asked.

"It's Mrs Ramsay reading to James," she said.

She knew his objection—that no one could tell it was a human shape.

"But I've made no attempt[16] at likeness," she said.

"Why did you introduce[17] them then?" he asked.

---

7 domineering [ˌdɑmə'nɪrɪŋ] (a.) 強勢的
8 insist [ɪn'sɪst] (v.) 堅持
9 dare [dɛr] (v.) 敢；竟敢
10 raise [rez] (v.) 舉起
11 narrow ['næro] (v.) 縮小
12 wince [wɪns] (v.) 退縮

13 trial ['traɪəl] (n.) 審判
14 penknife ['pɛnˌnaɪf] (n.) 小刀
15 tap [tæp] (v.) 輕敲
16 handle ['hændl] (n.) 刀柄
17 attempt [ə'tɛmpt] (n.) 企圖
18 introduce [ˌɪntrə'djus] (v.) 放入

The painting

- What is Lily painting?

  ☐ A portrait of the Ramsay family

  ☐ The scene in front of her eyes

  ☐ A portrait of mother and son

Why indeed? — except that if there, in that corner, it was bright, here, in this, there should be darkness. Simple, obvious[1], ordinary[2], as it was, Mr Bankes was interested.

Mother and child — objects of universal[3] respect, and in this case the mother was famous for her beauty — could be reduced[4] to a purple shadow.

He was interested. Somebody had seen her painting. This man had shared something very intimate[5] with her. She thanked Mr Ramsay for it and Mrs Ramsay for it, and the hour and the place. She was not alone any more. Now she could walk down that long gallery[6] arm in arm[7] with somebody. It was the strangest feeling in the world.

She shut her paint box and captured[8] in a vision[9] forever the paint box, the lawn, Mr Bankes and that wild child, Cam, running past.

Cam knocked the easel as she ran past. She would not stop for Mr Bankes and Lily Briscoe. She would not stop for her father; nor for her mother, who called, "Cam! I want you a moment!"

She was off like a bird, a bullet[10], or an arrow[11]. But when Mrs Ramsay called "Cam!" a second time, she stopped, and ran to her mother.

---

1 obvious [ˈɑbvɪəs] (a.) 清楚的
2 ordinary [ˈɔrdṇˌɛrɪ] (a.) 一般的
3 universal [ˌjunəˈvɜsl] (a.) 普遍的
4 reduce [rɪˈdjus] (v.) 簡化
5 intimate [ˈɪntəmɪt] (a.) 親密的
6 gallery [ˈgælərɪ] (n.) 畫廊
7 arm in arm 臂挽著臂
8 capture [ˈkæptʃə] (v.) 捕獲
9 vision [ˈvɪʒən] (n.) 所見之物
10 bullet [ˈbʊlɪt] (n.) 子彈
11 arrow [ˈæro] (n.) 箭

Mrs Ramsay had to repeat the question twice. "Have Andrew, Miss Doyle, and Mr Rayley come back?" Cam replied, "No, they haven't."

"Minta Doyle and Paul Rayley haven't come back. That can only mean one thing," Mrs Ramsay thought. "Minta has decided, rightly, to marry Paul Rayley."

He was not brilliant, but then, thought Mrs Ramsay, she preferred ordinary men to clever men who wrote dissertations; Charles Tansley, for example. "Anyhow he must have proposed[1], by now."

Here she was, making Minta marry Paul Rayley. Why was she always saying that people must marry, people must have children? Was it an escape for her?

"Am I wrong to say this?" she asked herself. "Minta is only twenty-four. Marriage needs all sorts of qualities. Has she got them? And where are they now?" Mrs Ramsay wondered. "And when will they tell me?" She was responsible[2] to Minta's parents. "Dear, dear," Mrs Ramsay said to herself, "how did they produce this tomboy[3] Minta?"

Of course, she had asked Minta to lunch, tea, dinner, finally to stay with them up at Finlay. This had resulted[4] in an argument[5] with Minta's mother. Another woman had once accused[6] her of "robbing her of her daughter's affections[7]". Interfering[8], making people do what she wished—that was the charge[9] against her, and she thought it very unjust. She was not domineering, nor was she tyrannical. She was more interested in hospitals and drains and the dairy[10] than she was in other people's children.

No hospital on the whole island. Milk delivered[11] at your door brown with dirt. It should be illegal[12].

"A model[13] dairy and a hospital up here — I'd like to organize[14] those two things. But how? With all these children? When they're older — then perhaps I'll have time — when they're all at school."

Oh, but she never wanted James to grow a day older or Cam either! She would like to keep these two just as they were, demons[15] of wickedness[16], angels of delight. James was the most gifted[17], the most sensitive of her children. But all her children were full of promise[18], she thought.

---

1 propose [prə'poz] (v.) 求婚
2 responsible [rɪ'spɑnsəbl] (a.) 負責任的
3 tomboy ['tɑm,bɔɪ] (n.) 男孩子氣的女孩
4 result [rɪ'zʌlt] (v.) 造成
5 argument ['ɑrgjəmənt] (n.) 爭吵
6 accuse [ə'kjuz] (v.) 指控
7 affection [ə'fɛkʃən] (n.) 感情
8 interfere [,ɪntə'fɪr] (v.) 介入；干涉
9 charge [tʃɑrdʒ] (n.) 控訴
10 dairy ['dɛrɪ] (n.) 乳品農場
11 deliver [dɪ'lɪvə] (v.) 遞送
12 illegal [ɪ'ligl] (a.) 非法的
13 model ['mɑdl] (a.) 模範的
14 organize ['ɔrgə,naɪz] (v.) 組織
15 demon ['dimən] (n.) 惡魔
16 wickedness ['wɪkɪdnɪs] (n.) 惡事
17 gifted ['gɪftɪd] (a.) 有天賦的
18 full of promise 充滿前途的

Prue took your breath away[1] with her beauty. Andrew — even her husband admitted[2] that his gift for mathematics was extraordinary. And Nancy and Roger, they were both wild creatures[3] now. They played in the fields all day long. As for Rose, her mouth was too big, but she was very good at making things. She did not like it that Jasper liked shooting[4] at birds; but it was only a stage[5]. They all went through stages.

She rested her chin on James's head. Why did they have to grow up so fast? Why did they have to go to school? She would like to always have a baby. She was happiest carrying a baby in her arms. And, kissing James on the head, she thought, "He will never be so happy again." Then she remembered how it annoyed her husband when she said that. "Still, it's true. They're happier now than they'll ever be again."

A ten-penny tea set makes Cam happy for days. And when she went up to say good night to them, they were all excited about the little treasures they had found in the garden or on the beach — a crab[6], a stone.

And so one night, she had gone downstairs and said to her husband, "Why must they grow up? They will never be so happy again."

And he was angry. "Why take such a gloomy[7] view of life?" he said. It was odd[8]; but she believed it to be true; he was happier and more hopeful than she was. Perhaps that was because he had his work.

1 take one's breath away 令人驚嘆
2 admit [əd`mɪt] (v.) 承認
3 creature [`kritʃɚ] (n.) 傢伙
4 shooting [`ʃutɪŋ] (n.) 射擊
5 stage [stedʒ] (n.) 階段
6 crab [kræb] (n.) 蟹
7 gloomy [`glumɪ] (a.) 陰鬱的
8 odd [ɑd] (a.) 奇怪的

It was getting late. She was worried about something. She could not remember what. Then she remembered; Paul and Minta and Andrew had not come back. She remembered the little group on the terrace, ready to go.

Andrew had his fishing net and basket. He was going to catch crabs and things. He'll climb onto a rock; he'll be cut off[1]. Or walking back on one of those little paths above the cliff[2], one of them might fall. It was growing dark.

She finished the story, she was reading to James. "And that's the end," she said.

Then she looked across the bay, and there, coming across the waves was the light from the Lighthouse. It had been lit[3]. James was looking at it too.

"In a moment he'll ask me, 'Are we going to the Lighthouse?' And I'll have to say, 'No, not tomorrow. Your father says no'."

Happily, Mildred came in to get James.

But he kept looking back over his shoulder as Mildred carried him out, and she was sure that he was thinking, "We're not going to the Lighthouse tomorrow." And she thought, "He'll remember that all his life."

No, she thought, looking at the pictures he had cut out — a refrigerator, a lawn mower, a gentleman in evening dress[4] — children never forget.

1 cut off 切斷
2 cliff [klɪf] (n.) 懸崖；峭壁
3 light [laɪt] (v.) 點燃（動詞三態：light; lighted, lit; lighted, lit）
4 evening dress 晚禮服

Children

- Do you agree that children never forget?
  Make a list of your childhood memories:

  - [ ] An excursion you went on
  - [ ] A person you met
  - [ ] A special moment

For this reason, it was so important what you said, and what you did. And it was a relief[1] when they went to bed. Then she didn't need to think about anybody. She could be herself.

She looked at the long steady stroke[2] of the Lighthouse, the last of the three, which was her stroke. She felt calm again.

She returned to her knitting. "How can any god have made this world?" she asked. "There's no reason, order or justice. There's only suffering[3], death, the poor. No happiness lasts." She knew that.

When her husband passed, he noticed her seriousness[4], and it upset him. He felt that he could not protect[5] her. And, when he reached the hedge, he was sad. He could do nothing to help her. In fact, he made things worse for her. He was bad-tempered. He had lost his temper over the Lighthouse. He looked into the hedge, into its darkness.

Then he turned and saw her again. Ah! She was lovely, lovelier now than ever, he thought. He wanted to speak to her now that James had gone and she was alone at last. But he decided not to. He could not interrupt her.

He passed her without a word, though it hurt him that she looked so sad and distant, and he could not reach her. He could do nothing to help her. He walked past her again. She called to him, and walked over to him. For she knew he wanted to protect her.

She took his arm. There was a ladder against the greenhouse, because they were beginning to mend[6] the greenhouse. She was about to say, "It'll cost fifty pounds." But instead, she talked about Jasper shooting birds.

He said, "It's natural for a boy. He'll soon find better ways of amusing himself."

Her husband was so sensible, so just. And so she said, "Yes, all children go through stages," and began looking at the flowers.

Thoughts

- Do these two people tell each other their secret thoughts?
- Do you tell anybody what you are really thinking?

1 relief [rɪˈlif] (n.) 緩和；解除
2 stroke [strok] (n.) 一連串機械動作中的一個動作
3 suffering [ˈsʌfərɪŋ] (n.) 受苦
4 seriousness [ˈsɪrɪəsnɪs] (n.) 嚴肅
5 protect [prəˈtɛkt] (v.) 保護
6 mend [mɛnd] (v.) 修理

"Have you heard the children's nickname for Charles Tansley?" she asked. "The atheist, they call him, the little atheist. Pray[1] Heaven[2] he won't fall in love with Prue," said Mrs Ramsay.

"I'll disinherit[3] her if she marries him," said Mr Ramsay. "But Tansley's harmless," he added.

They walked along, towards the red-hot pokers. "You're teaching your daughters to exaggerate[4]," said Mr Ramsay, reproving[5] her.

"Aunt Camilla was far worse than me," Mrs Ramsay remarked[6].

"Nobody ever held up your Aunt Camilla as an example[7]," said Mr Ramsay.

"She was the most beautiful woman I ever saw," said Mrs Ramsay.

"Somebody else was that," said Mr Ramsay.

"Prue is going to be far more beautiful than I was," said Mrs Ramsay.

"I don't think so," said Mr Ramsay.

"Well, then, look tonight," said Mrs Ramsay.

They paused.

"I wish Andrew would work harder. He won't get a scholarship[8] if he doesn't," he said.

"Oh, scholarships!" she said.

"I'll be very proud of Andrew if he gets a scholarship," Mr Ramsay said.

"I'll be just as proud of him if he doesn't," she answered.

---

1 pray [pre] (v.) 祈求
2 Heaven ['hɛvən] (n.) 上帝
3 disinherit [,dɪsɪn'hɛrɪt] (v.) 剝奪繼承權
4 exaggerate [ɪg'zædʒə,ret] (v.) 誇大

They always disagreed about this, but it did not matter. She liked him to believe in scholarships, and he liked her to be proud of Andrew whatever he did.

Suddenly she remembered those little paths on the edge of the cliffs.

"Isn't it late?" she asked. "They haven't come home yet."

He looked at his watch. "But it's only seven o'clock."

They had reached the gap between the red-hot pokers, and there was the Lighthouse again, but she did not look at it.

It was silly to be worried about Andrew. When he was Andrew's age, he used to[9] walk about the country all day long. Nobody worried about him, or thought that he had fallen over a cliff.

She worried about the boys, but not about him.

Years ago, before he had married, he thought, looking across the bay, he had walked all day. You could walk all day without meeting anyone. There were very few houses, and no villages for miles on end[10]. You could think.

He sometimes thought that in a little house out there, alone — he stopped and sighed. He had no right. He was the father of eight children — he reminded himself. "I would be a beast to want to change a single thing," he thought. "Andrew will be a better man than I am. Prue will be a beauty, her mother says. That's a good bit of work — my eight children."

---

5 reprove [rɪˈpruv] (v.) 非難
6 remark [rɪˈmɑrk] (v.) 評論
7 hold up sb as an example 把某人當作模範
8 scholarship [ˈskɑləˌʃɪp] (n.) 獎學金
9 used to 以前常常……
10 for miles on end 在很遠的距離內

He sighed again.

She heard him. "What are you sighing about?" she asked.

She guessed what he was thinking — he would have written better books if he had not married.

"I'm not complaining," he said.

And he took her hand and kissed it with an intensity[1] that brought tears to her eyes. Quickly, he dropped it. She knew that he wasn't complaining. She knew that he had nothing to complain about.

They turned away from the view and began to walk up the path arm in arm. "He was made differently from other people," she thought. "He was born blind, deaf, and dumb[2] to the ordinary things. But to the extraordinary things, he has an eagle's eye. Does he notice the flowers? No. Does he notice the view? No. Does he even notice whether there's pudding[3] on his plate or roast beef? He sits at the table with us like a person in a dream."

At that moment, he said, "Very fine," to please her. He was pretending to admire the flowers. But she knew that he did not admire them, or even notice that they were there. It was only to please her.

She saw a couple ahead of them on the path. "Ah, but isn't that Lily Briscoe walking along with William Bankes?" she thought. "Yes, it is. Doesn't that mean that they'll marry? Yes, it does! What a good idea! They must marry!"

Lily Briscoe and Mr Bankes were talking about art. There were lots of paintings Lily had not seen. "Perhaps it's better not to see paintings," she said. "They only make me very unhappy with my own work."

1　intensity [ɪnˈtɛnsətɪ] (n.) 強烈；熱烈
2　dumb [dʌm] (a.) 啞的
3　pudding [ˈpʊdɪŋ] 指約克夏布甸（Yorkshire pudding），
　　一種英國料理，為烤牛肉的配菜

"We can't all be Titians[1] and we can't all be Darwins[2]," Mr Bankes said. "But can you have a Darwin or a Titian if you don't have ordinary people like ourselves?"

Lily wanted to pay him a compliment[3]. "You're not ordinary, Mr Bankes."

But he did not want compliments (most men do, she thought). As they reached the end of the lawn, they turned and saw the Ramsays.

"So, that's marriage," Lily thought. "A man and a woman watching a girl throwing a ball."

For they were standing close together watching Prue and Jasper throwing and catching a ball. And suddenly they were the symbols of marriage, husband and wife.

Mrs Ramsay greeted them with a smile (oh, she's thinking we're going to get married, Lily thought) and she said, "Mr Bankes has agreed to dine with us tonight."

The ball soared[4] high. They followed it and lost it and saw the one star.

Prue ran and caught the ball, and her mother said, "Haven't they come back yet? Did Nancy go with them?"

Nancy had gone with them. Minta Doyle had asked her to. She did not want to go but she went.

---

1 Titan [ˈtaɪtn̩] (n.) 傑出的人物
2 Darwin [ˈdɑrwɪn] 達爾文（提出演化論的英國生物學家）
3 compliment [ˈkɑmpləmənt] (n.) 讚美的話
4 soar [sor] (v.) 高飛
5 cast [kæst] (v.) 投擲（動詞三態：cast; cast; cast）
6 tiny [ˈtaɪnɪ] (a.) 微小的
7 desolation [ˌdɛslˈeʃən] (n.) 荒涼
8 innocent [ˈɪnəsn̩t] (a.) 無罪的
9 stream [strim] (v.) 流瀉
10 heavens [ˈhɛvəns] (int.) （感嘆詞）天啊
11 outraged [ˈaʊtˌredʒɪd] (a.) 憤慨的

When they got to the beach, they separated. Andrew went to look for crabs, and left the couple alone. Nancy sat by a rock pool, and let the couple alone, too. She changed the pool into the sea, and made the little fish into sharks and whales. She cast[5] huge clouds over this tiny[6] world by holding her hand against the sun. She brought darkness and desolation[7], like God himself, to millions of innocent[8] creatures. Then she took her hand away suddenly and let the sun stream[9] down.

"The sea's coming in," Andrew shouted.

So Nancy ran up the beach and behind a rock and there — oh, heavens[10]! in each other's arms, were Paul and Minta, kissing probably. She was outraged[11]. She and Andrew put on their shoes and socks in silence without saying a thing about it.

🎧 "Yes," said Prue, answering her mother's question, "I think Nancy did go with them."

So, Nancy went with them, thought Mrs Ramsay. There was a tap at the door. Mrs Ramsay put down her hairbrush[1], and said, "Come in."

Jasper and Rose came in. Did the fact that Nancy was with them make it less likely or more likely that something had happened? It made it less likely, Mrs Ramsay decided. They could not all have drowned.

"Rose, which jewelry[2] shall I wear?" she asked.

Jasper offered[3] her an opal[4] necklace; Rose a gold necklace. Which looked best against her black dress?

"Choose, dearests, choose," she said.

She let them take their time to choose. She let Rose look at this necklace and then that, and hold them against the black dress. She knew that Rose loved this little ceremony[5] of choosing jewelry. They went through it every night.

Suddenly they heard the great clang[6] of the gong[7]. It announced[8] that all those scattered[9] about, in attics[10], in bedrooms, reading, writing, or brushing their hair must leave all that, and go to the dining room for dinner.

"I'm ready now to go down to dinner," said Mrs Ramsay.

---

1 hairbrush [ˋhɛr͵brʌʃ] (n.) 髮刷
2 jewelry [ˋdʒuəlrɪ] (n.) (總稱) 珠寶
3 offer [ˋɔfɚ] (v.) 提供
4 opal [ˋopḷ] (n.) 蛋白石
5 ceremony [ˋsɛrə͵monɪ] (n.) 典禮

6 clang [klæŋ] (n.) 鏗鏘聲
7 gong [gɔŋ] (n.) 鑼
8 announce [əˋnauns] (v.) 宣布
9 scatter [ˋskætɚ] (v.) 分布
10 attic [ˋætɪk] (n.) 閣樓

"But what have I done with my life?" thought Mrs Ramsay, sitting down at the head of the table. "William, sit by me," she said. "Lily," she said, tiredly, "sit over there."

It was as if a shadow had fallen, and, robbed everything of color. The room (she looked round it) was very shabby. There was no beauty anywhere. Quickly, she gave herself a little shake like you give a watch that has stopped. Then she turned to William Bankes — poor man! He had no wife and no children and he dined alone. In pity for him, she began the business of conversation.

"Did you find your letters? Mildred put them in the hall for you," she said to William Bankes.

Lily Briscoe watched her. "How old she looks," Lily thought. "And why does she pity William Bankes? It was one of those misjudgments[1] of hers. He isn't pitiable[2]. He has his work," Lily said to herself. And she had her work, too.

Suddenly, she saw her painting, and thought, "Yes, I'll put the tree in the middle. That's what I'll do. That's what's been puzzling[3] me."

She picked up the salt pot and put it down on a flower pattern[4] on the tablecloth, to remind herself to move the tree.

"It's odd that you hardly ever get anything important in the post, but you always want a letter," said Mr Bankes.

"What nonsense they talk," thought Charles Tansley.

"Do you write many letters, Mr Tansley?" asked Mrs Ramsay. She pities him too, Lily thought.

"I write to my mother," said Mr Tansley. He wasn't going to talk the sort of nonsense these silly women talked about.

He had been reading in his room, and now this all seemed silly. Why did they dress for dinner? He had come down in his ordinary clothes. They did nothing but talk, talk, talk, eat, eat, eat. It was the women's fault. Women made civilization impossible with all their silliness.

"We won't be able to go to the Lighthouse tomorrow, Mrs Ramsay," he said.

He liked her; he admired her; but he felt it necessary to say this.

"He was the most uncharming[5] man she had ever met," Lily Briscoe thought. Then why did she mind what he said? "Women can't write; women can't paint."

"Oh, Mr Tansley," she said, "do take me to the Lighthouse with you. I'd love to go."

She was telling lies. He knew that. She was laughing at him. He felt very lonely. She didn't want to go to the Lighthouse with him. She despised[6] him; so did Prue Ramsay; so did they all. But he was not going to be made a fool of by women, so he turned and looked out of the window. Then he said, very rudely, "It will be too rough[7] for you tomorrow. You'll be sick."

---

1 misjudgment [mɪsˋdʒʌdʒmənt] (n.) 判斷錯誤
2 pitiable [ˋpɪtɪəbl̩] (a.) 令人憐憫的
3 puzzle [ˋpʌzl̩] (v.) 困惑
4 pattern [ˋpætɚn] (n.) 圖案
5 uncharming [ʌnˋtʃɑrmɪŋ] (a.) 不迷人的
6 despise [dɪˋspaɪz] (v.) 鄙視；看不起
7 rough [rʌf] (a.) 風大的

Then he turned to talk to Mrs Ramsay. But Mrs Ramsay was talking to William Bankes.

"I wish I hadn't come," thought Mr Bankes. "I could have worked."

"How you must hate dining in this bear garden[1]," Mrs Ramsay said.

Mr Bankes said, "No, not at all."

"He's lying," thought Mr Tansley. "The Ramsays talk nonsense," he thought. It was worthwhile staying with them once, but not again. The women were boring. And of course Ramsay had burnt his boats[2] by marrying a beautiful woman and having eight children.

"They must come now," Mrs Ramsay thought, looking at the door.

And just then, Minta Doyle, Paul Rayley and a maid, carrying a big dish in her hands, came in together.

"We're awfully late," Minta said, as they walked to different ends of the table.

"I lost my brooch[3] — my grandmother's brooch," said Minta in a sad voice, with a sad look in her big brown eyes, as she sat next to Mr Ramsay.

"How could you be such a goose[4]," he asked, "as to climb over the rocks in jewels?"

---

1 bear garden 人聲吵雜的地方
2 burn one's boats 自斷退路
3 brooch [brotʃ] (n.) 女用胸針
4 goose [gus] (n.) 笨蛋

5 engaged [ɪnˋgedʒd] (a.) 訂了婚的
6 olive [ˋɑlɪv] (n.) 橄欖
7 recipe [ˋrɛsəpɪ] (n.) 食譜
8 fade [fed] (v.) 遜色

"It must have happened then," thought Mrs Ramsay. "They're engaged[5]. Paul must sit next to me. I've kept a place for him."

"We went back to look for Minta's brooch," he said, sitting down next to Mrs Ramsay.

"We" — that was enough. She knew that it was the first time he had said "we". We did this; we did that. "They'll say that all their lives," she thought.

Just then a wonderful smell of olives[6] rose from the great brown dish as the maid took the lid off. The cook had spent three days over that dish.

"It's delicious," said Mr Bankes.

"It's a French recipe[7] of my grandmother's," said Mrs Ramsay.

"Where did Minta lose her brooch?" Lily asked.

"On the beach," Paul said. "I'm going to find it tomorrow."

Lily, in her little gray dress with her pale face and her little Chinese eyes faded[8], under Minta's glow[9].

"Everything about her is so small. Yet," thought Mrs Ramsay, comparing[10] her with Minta, "Lily at forty will look better than Minta. There's something in Lily which I really like, but no man will like, I fear. Unless it's a much older man, like William Bankes. William must marry Lily. They have so many things in common[11]. They are both fond of flowers. They are both cold and unfriendly. I must arrange for them to take a long walk together." Foolishly[12], she had placed them opposite each other. "I'll put that right tomorrow. If it's fine, we'll go for a picnic," she thought. Everything seemed possible. Everything seemed right.

---

9 glow [glo] (n.) 光芒
10 compare [kəm`pɛr] (v.) 比較
11 in common 共有的
12 foolishly [`fulɪʃlɪ] (adv.) 愚蠢地

She put her spoon down, and listened to her husband. He was talking about the square root[1] of one thousand two hundred and fifty-three. What did it all mean? To this day she had no idea. A square root? What was that? Her sons knew. Cubes[2] and square roots; that was what they were talking about now. Men were so clever. Then William Bankes was praising the Waverley novels[3].

"Ah, but how long do you think their popularity[4] will last?" asked somebody.

Mrs Ramsay smelt danger for her husband. "A question like this will remind him of his own failure," she thought. ""How long will I be read?" he'll think."

William Bankes (who was free from all such vanity[5]) laughed, and said, "Changes in fashion aren't important. Who can tell what's going to last in literature[6] or in anything else? Let's enjoy what we enjoy," he said.

Mrs Ramsay knew that Mr Ramsay was beginning to feel uneasy. He wanted somebody to say, "Oh, but your work will last, Mr Ramsay," or something like that.

He said that Scott (or was it Shakespeare?) would last him his lifetime. He said it irritably[7]. Everybody, she thought, felt a little uncomfortable.

Then Minta Doyle, said, "I don't believe that anyone really enjoys reading Shakespeare."

1 square root 平方根
2 cube [kjub] (n.) 立方
3 《威弗萊》（*Waverley*）是 1814 年出版、廣受歡迎的歷史小說，作者後來的小說被標為「由《威弗萊》的作者縮寫」，其在同一時期寫的同類小說，就被稱為「威弗萊系列小說」（Waverley novels）
4 popularity [ˌpɑpjəˈlærətɪ] (n.) 廣受歡迎
5 vanity [ˈvænətɪ] (n.) 虛榮
6 literature [ˈlɪtərətʃɚ] (n.) 文學
7 irritably [ˈɪrətəblɪ] (adv.) 急躁地

Mr Ramsay said, "Very few people like it as much as they say they do. But," he added, "some of his plays are very good."

And Mrs Ramsay saw that it would be all right for the moment anyhow. "He'll laugh at Minta. And she'll praise him, somehow or other[1]."

Then she looked at her children. Prue kept looking at Minta, curiously. Mrs Ramsay thought, "You'll be as happy as Minta is one of these days." "You'll be much happier," she added, "because you're my daughter." Her own daughter must be happier than other people's daughters.

Dinner was over at last. They all left the dining room. Mrs Ramsay stood in the hallway for a few minutes to look out of the window. It was windy.

"However long they live, they'll remember this night; this moon; this wind; this house; and me too," she thought and it made her happy. "However long they live, I'll have a place in their hearts."

She smiled and went into the other room, where her husband sat reading.

She looked at her husband (as she picked up her sock and began to knit), and saw that he did not want to be interrupted. He was reading something that moved him very much. It was one of Sir Walter Scott's novels, she saw.

For Charles Tansley had been saying that people don't read Scott any more. Then her husband thought, "That's what they'll say about me." So he went and got one of Scott's books. He was always worrying about his books — will people read them, are they good, what do people think of me?

She continued knitting and wondering. Then she looked across at her husband. Their eyes met for a second; but they did not want to speak to each other. Don't interrupt me, he seemed to be saying. Don't say anything; just sit there. And he went on reading. It was a wonderful book. It filled[2] him. It strengthened him. He forgot all the little annoyances[3] of the evening. He let the tears fall. He forgot his own worries and failures completely as he read (this was Sir Walter Scott at his best).

---

1 somehow or other 以某種方法；不知怎地
2 fill [fɪl] (v.) 充滿；滿足
3 annoyance [əˈnɔɪəns] (n.) 討厭的物或人

"Well, let them improve[1] on that," he thought as he finished the chapter. They could not improve on that. If young men did not care for this book, then of course, they did not care for his books either. He looked at his wife. She was reading now. She looked very peaceful, reading. He liked sitting alone with her.

Mrs Ramsay became aware of[2] her husband looking at her. He was smiling at her, and he was thinking, "Go on reading. You don't look sad now."

And he wondered what she was reading. He liked to think that she was not clever, not book-learned[3] at all. He wondered if she understood what she was reading. Probably not, he thought. She was very beautiful.

"Well?" she said, putting her book down. "They're engaged," she said, beginning to knit, "Paul and Minta."

"So I guessed," he said.

There was nothing very much to say about it. She was still thinking about the poetry. He was still feeling very emotional, after reading his book. So they sat silent.

He was still looking at her, but his look had changed. He wanted her to tell him that she loved him. And she couldn't do that. He found talking so much easier than she did. He could say things — she never could. He called her a heartless[4] woman.

She got up and stood by the window with the brown sock in her hands, partly to turn away from him, partly because she remembered how beautiful it often is — the sea at night. But she knew that he was watching her. She knew that he was thinking, "You are more beautiful than ever."

And she felt very beautiful.

"Will you not tell me that you love me?"

But she could not say it.

Then, instead of saying anything, she turned and looked at him. And as she looked at him, she began to smile.

And he knew that she loved him. He could not deny[5] it.

And smiling she looked out of the window and said to herself, "Nothing on earth[6] can equal this happiness."

---

1 improve [ɪmˋpruv] (v.) 增進；改善
2 become aware of 注意到
3 book-learned [ˋbʊkˋlɝnɪd] (a.) 有學識的
4 heartless [ˋhɑrtlɪs] (a.) 無動於衷的
5 deny [dɪˋnaɪ] (v.) 否認
6 on earth 人世間

II. TIME PASSES

The nights now are full of wind and destruction[1]. The trees plunge[2] and bend, and their leaves fly helter-skelter[3] until the lawn is covered with them. They lie packed[4] in gutters[5] and choked[6] rain pipes[7] and scatter[8] across paths.

Mr Ramsay, stumbling[9] along a passage[10] one dark morning, stretched[11] his arms out. Mrs Ramsay had died suddenly the night before. His arms remained empty.

So, with the house empty and the doors locked, curtains flapped[12], wood creaked[13], pans and china[14] cracked[15].

The spring came and Prue Ramsay got married. People said how beautiful she looked!

But sadly, Prue Ramsay died that summer in an illness connected with childbirth[16]. It was a tragedy, people said. Everything, they said, had promised so well.

---

1 destruction [dɪˋstrʌkʃən] (n.) 毀滅
2 plunge [plʌndʒ] (v.) 使投入
3 helter-skelter [ˋhɛltɚˏskɛltɚ] (adv.) 倉皇地
4 pack [pæk] (v.) 塞滿
5 gutter [ˋgʌtɚ] (n.) 排水溝
6 choke [tʃok] (v.) 堵塞
7 rain pipe 排水管
8 scatter [ˋskætɚ] (v.) 散布

9 stumble [ˋstʌmbl̩] (v.) 蹣跚而行
10 passage [ˋpæsɪdʒ] (n.) 通道
11 stretch [strɛtʃ] (v.) 伸出
12 flap [flæp] (v.) 飄動
13 creak [krik] (v.) 使咯吱作響
14 china [ˋtʃaɪnə] (n.) 瓷器
15 crack [kræk] (v.) 破裂縫
16 childbirth [ˋtʃaɪldˏbɝθ] (n.) 分娩

Later in the summer, there were ominous[1] sounds, like the blows[2] of hammers. Now and again some glass tinkled[3] in the cupboard as if a giant voice had cried so loud in agony[4] that it shook the glass. Then again silence fell; and then, night after night and sometimes in the middle of the day, there was the thud[5] of something falling.

A shell[6] exploded[7]. Twenty or thirty young men were blown up[8] in France, among them Andrew Ramsay. Mercifully[9], his death was instant. There was a purplish stain[10] upon the surface of the sea now, as if something had boiled and bled[11], invisibly[12], beneath.

Time

- **What happens to the Ramsay family as "time passes"?**

  Mrs Ramsay _____

  Prue _____

  Andrew_____

1 ominous [`ɑmɪnəs] (a.) 凶兆的
2 blow [blo] (n.) 重擊
3 tinkle [`tɪŋkl̩] (v.) 作叮鈴聲
4 agony [`ægənɪ] (n.) 極度痛苦
5 thud [θʌd] (n.) 砰的一聲
6 shell [ʃɛl] (n.) 砲彈
7 explode [ɪk`splod] (v.) 爆炸

8 blow up 炸毀
9 mercifully [`mɝsɪfəlɪ] (adv.) 仁慈地
10 stain [sten] (n.) 污跡
11 bleed [blid] (v.) 流血（動詞三態：
    bleed; bled; bled）
12 invisibly [ɪn`vɪzəblɪ] (adv.) 看不見地

Mr Carmichael brought out[1] a book of poems[2] that spring. It was very successful. The War, people said, had revived[3] their interest in poetry[4].

"The family will never come to the house again," people said. "The house will be sold in the autumn perhaps."

There were clothes in the bedroom cupboards. "What shall I do with do them?" thought Mrs McNab. "And Mrs Ramsay's things. Poor lady! She'll never need *them* again. She's dead, they say; years ago, in London." There was the old gray cloak[5] she wore for gardening (Mrs McNab looked at it).

She could see her, as she came up the drive with the washing, looking at her flowers. There were boots[6] and shoes; and a brush and comb left on the dressing-table[7]. "It's as if she expects to come back tomorrow," she thought. (She had died very suddenly, they said.)

Because of the War, they hadn't come to the house for years. Many things had changed. Many families had lost their loved ones. So Mrs Ramsay was dead; and Mr Andrew killed; and Miss Prue dead too, they said, with her first baby. But everyone had lost somebody during the War.

Then all of a sudden, one of the young ladies wrote and asked Mrs McNab to get the house ready. They might be coming for the summer; had left everything to the last minute; expected to find things as they had left them.

Slowly and painfully, with broom and bucket, mopping[8], scrubbing[9], Mrs McNab stopped the rot[10]. She rescued[11] from the pool of Time: a cupboard, a carpet, a tea set, the books. Finally, after days of hard work, the house was ready.

Lily Briscoe had her bag carried up to the house late one evening in September. Mr Carmichael came by the same train.

The curtains of dark wrapped[12] themselves over the house, over Mr Carmichael, and Lily Briscoe. The sigh of all the seas round the islands soothed[13] them. Nothing broke their sleep, until the sun lifted the curtains. Lily Briscoe opened her eyes. Here she was again, she thought, sitting up in bed.

1 bring out 出版
2 poem ['poɪm] (n.) (可數) 詩篇
3 revive [rɪ'vaɪv] (v.) 復甦
4 poetry ['poɪtrɪ] (n.) 〔總稱〕(不可數) 詩
5 cloak [klok] (n.) 斗篷;披風
6 boot [but] (n.) 靴子
7 dressing-table ['drɛsɪŋ'tebl̩] (n.) 梳妝台

8 mop [mɑp] (v.) 用拖把拖洗
9 scrub [skrʌb] (v.) 用力擦洗
10 rot [rɑt] (n.) 腐壞
11 rescue ['rɛskju] (v.) 營救
12 wrap [ræp] (v.) 包裹
13 soothe [suð] (v.) 安慰

III. THE LIGHTHOUSE

What did she feel, coming back here after all these years and Mrs Ramsay dead? Lily Briscoe asked herself. Nothing — nothing. She had come late last night when it was all mysterious[1] and dark. Now she was sitting at the breakfast table, alone. It was very early, not yet eight o'clock.

Mr Ramsay, Cam and James were going to the Lighthouse. They should have gone already — they had to catch the tide[2] or something. And Cam was not ready and James was not ready and Nancy had forgotten to order the sandwiches and Mr Ramsay had lost his temper[3] and banged[4] out of the room.

"What's the use of going now?" he said angrily.

Sitting alone among the clean cups at the long table, the house, the place, the morning, all seemed strangers to her. She had no attachment[5] here.

"How unreal it is," she thought, looking at her empty coffee cup. "Mrs Ramsay dead; Andrew killed; Prue dead too." But she didn't feel anything.

Suddenly Mr Ramsay raised his head as he passed the window, and looked straight at her, with his wild gaze. Lily pretended to drink from her empty coffee cup. She didn't want to talk to him.

eee nff.-

He shook his head at her, and walked on ("Alone," she heard him say, "Died," she heard him say). He wanted sympathy and she was not going to give him any.

Then suddenly she remembered. When she had sat here ten years ago, there had been a little leaf pattern on the tablecloth. There had been a problem with her picture. Move the tree to the middle, she had said. She had never finished that picture. "I'll paint that picture now," she thought. "Where are my paints?" she wondered. "I left them in the hall last night. I'll start at once."

She got up quickly, before Mr Ramsay returned.

She placed her easel on the lawn. "Yes, it was here that I stood ten years ago. There's the wall, the hedge, the tree," she thought. She had kept the picture in her mind all these years. And now she could finish it.

Lily's painting

- Look back at page 49. Who had commented on Lily's painting?
- Why hadn't she finished that picture?

1 mysterious [mɪsˈtɪrɪəs] (a.) 神祕的
2 tide [taɪd] (n.) 海潮
3 temper [ˈtɛmpɚ] (n.) 脾氣
4 bang [bæŋ] (v.) 發出砰的一聲
5 attachment [əˈtætʃmənt] (n.) 情感；忠誠

Lily set her clean canvas[1] on the easel. She did her best to look at her picture. But she couldn't.

"When will the children come? When will they leave for the Lighthouse?"

She wanted Mr Ramsay to go. Mr Ramsay, she thought, angrily, never gave; he took. Mrs Ramsay had given. Giving, giving, giving, she had died. It was all Mrs Ramsay's fault. She was dead. Here was Lily, at forty-four, wasting her time, standing there, playing at painting. It was all Mrs Ramsay's fault. She was dead. The step where she used to sit was empty. She was dead.

"They shouldn't have asked me. I shouldn't have come," she thought.

James and Cam walked onto the terrace, a serious, sad couple. Mr Ramsay had a rucksack[2] over his shoulders. Then he led the way down the path, with his children following him.

Lily stood and watched them go. "What a face," she thought. "What has made it like that? Thinking, night after night," she supposed, "about the reality of kitchen tables." She remembered the symbol, which Andrew had given her. (He was killed by a shell instantly, she thought.)

"Can't paint; can't write," she murmured. Charles Tansley used to say that, she remembered.

---

1 canvas ['kænvəs] (n.) 油畫布
2 rucksack ['rʌk‚sæk] (n.) 帆布背包

Then she remembered the scene[1] on the beach. It was a windy morning. They had all gone down to the beach. Mrs Ramsay sat by a rock and wrote letters. She wrote and wrote. Charles Tansley became as nice as he could possibly be. He played a game with Lily. Together they chose little flat black stones and sent them skipping[2] over the waves.

Every now and then Mrs Ramsay looked up and laughed at them. She remembered them getting on very well, and Mrs Ramsay watching them. Mrs Ramsay had made this scene on the beach, this moment of friendship and liking. It survived[3] complete, after all these years. It was like a work of art.

She must rest for a moment. And, resting, the old question came to her. What is the meaning of life? It was a simple question, but the answer had never come. The answer perhaps never comes. Instead there are little daily miracles[4], matches struck[5] in the dark. This was one. Herself and Charles Tansley and the sea; Mrs Ramsay bringing them together; Mrs Ramsay making something permanent[6] of that moment.

"Life stands still here," Mrs Ramsay said.

"Mrs Ramsay! Mrs Ramsay!" she repeated.

Lily stepped back to look at her picture. She dipped into[7] the blue paint. She dipped into the past too.

---

1 scene [sin] (n.) 景象
2 skip [skip] (v.) 跳過
3 survive [sə`vaɪv] (v.) 倖存
4 miracle [`mɪrək]] (n.) 奇蹟
5 strike [straɪk] (v.) 擦（火柴）（動詞三態：strike; struck; struck, stricken）
6 permanent [`pɜmənənt] (a.) 永遠的
7. dip into . . . 沉浸於……

Then Mrs Ramsay got up, she remembered. It was time to go back to the house — time for lunch. And they all walked up from the beach together. She walking behind with William Bankes, and Paul and Minta were in front of them.

"The Rayleys," thought Lily Briscoe, squeezing[1] her tube[2] of green paint. "Their marriage turned out badly. Things started to go wrong after the first year. They're no longer 'in love'. Paul had an affair[3] with another woman, a serious woman, who went to meetings and shared his views."

"So that's the story of the Rayleys," Lily thought. She imagined herself telling it to Mrs Ramsay. She would be very curious to know what had become of the Rayleys. Lily would enjoy telling Mrs Ramsay that the marriage had not been a success.

She'd tell her, "It has all gone against your wishes. They're happy like that; I'm happy like this. Life has changed completely." And for a moment, Mrs Ramsay became dusty[4] and out of date[5]. For a moment, Lily triumphed over Mrs Ramsay. "She'll never know that Paul has a mistress[6]. How I stand here painting, have never married, not even William Bankes."

Mrs Ramsay had planned their marriage. Perhaps, if she had lived, they would have got married. That summer he was "the kindest of men". He was "the first scientist of his age, my husband says". He was also "poor William — it makes me so unhappy, when I go to see him. There's nothing in his house — no one to arrange the flowers."

---

1 squeeze [skwiz] (v.) 擠
2 tube [tjub] (n.) （顏料）管
3 affair [əˋfɛr] (n.) 戀情
4 dusty [ˋdʌstɪ] (a.) 滿佈塵埃的
5 out of date 過時的
6 mistress [ˋmɪstrɪs] (n.) 情婦

So she sent them for walks together. "What was that mania[7] of hers for marriage?" Lily wondered, looking at her painting. "She had only escaped by the skin of her teeth[8]," she thought. She had looked at the tablecloth, and realized that she needed to move the tree to the middle. She didn't need to marry anybody. She suddenly felt an enormous[9] happiness. "Now I can stand up to[10] Mrs Ramsay," she thought.

In fact William Bankes's friendship had been one of the pleasures of her life. She loved William Bankes.

Mr Carmichael lay on his chair with his hands on his stomach. His book had fallen on to the grass.

"What does it all mean?" she wanted to ask Mr Carmichael, but she didn't.

She looked at her picture. That was his answer, she thought. Nothing stays. Everything changes. But not words, not paint. Pictures remained forever.

Her eyes filled with tears, which rolled down her cheeks. She was crying for Mrs Ramsay.

She looked at old Mr Carmichael again. For one moment she felt that if they both got up, and demanded an explanation: "Why is life so short? Why is it so inexplicable[11]?" The space would fill; a shape would form. If they shouted loud enough, Mrs Ramsay would return.

"Mrs Ramsay!" she said aloud, "Mrs Ramsay!" The tears ran down her face.

---

7 mania [ˈmenɪə] (n.) 狂熱
8 by the skin of one's teeth 虎口脫險
9 enormous [ɪˈnɔrməs] (a.) 巨大的
10 stand up to 勇敢地面對
11 inexplicable [ɪnˈɛksplɪkəbl] (a.) 難了解的

And what had happened to Charles Tansley, she wondered. He had got his fellowship. He had married. He lived in Golder's Green. She had gone one day into a hall and heard him speaking during the war. He was denouncing[1] something: he was condemning[2] somebody.

Suddenly the boat came to a stop, in the hot sun, miles from the Lighthouse.

Mr Ramsay was reading a book. And all the time, as his father read, James dreaded[3] the moment when he would look up and ask, "Why are we sitting here?"

"And if he does," James thought, "then I shall take a knife and stab[4] him through the heart."

He had always kept this old symbol of taking a knife and stabbing his father through the heart. Only now he thought, "It's not really this old man that I want to kill. I just want to fight and stamp out[5] bullying[6]." "It will rain," he remembered his father saying. "You won't be able to go to the Lighthouse."

The sail swung[7] round. The boat woke up and shot[8] through the waves. Mr Ramsay sat there with the wind blowing his hair about.

"He looked very old," James thought.

"I'm hungry," said Mr Ramsay, suddenly shutting his book. "It's time for lunch. Besides, look," he said. "There's the Lighthouse. We're almost there."

---

1 denounce [dɪˈnaʊns] (v.) 指責
2 condemn [kənˈdɛm] (v.) 譴責
3 dread [drɛd] (v.) 懼怕
4 stab [stæb] (v.) 刺
5 stamp out 擺脫
6 bullying [ˈbʊlɪɪŋ] (n.) 欺凌
7 swing [swɪŋ] (v.) 擺動（動態三態：swing; swung; swung）
8 shoot [ʃut] (v.) 急速通過（動態三態：shoot; shot; shot）

"He's doing very well," said Macalister, the old boatman[1], praising James. "He's keeping the boat very steady[2]."

But his father never praised him, James thought angrily.

Mr Ramsay opened the parcel[3] and shared out the sandwiches. Then he said triumphantly[4], "Well done, James! You've steered[5] the boat like a real sailor."

"There!" Cam thought, addressing herself silently to James. "You've got it at last." For she knew that this was what James wanted. His father had praised him.

Now they could see two men on the Lighthouse, watching them and preparing to meet them.

Mr Ramsay put on his hat. "Bring those parcels," he said.

"He must have reached the Lighthouse," said Lily Briscoe. And suddenly she felt very tired.

"He has landed[6]," she said. "It's finished."

Quickly, she turned to her picture. There it was, with all its greens and blues. "It'll hang in an attic," she thought. "But what does that matter?"

She looked at the steps; they were empty. She looked at the picture. Then she drew[7] a line in the center. It was done; it was finished.

"Yes", she thought, laying down her brush exhausted, "I've had my vision."

---

1 boatman ['botmən] (n.) 船夫
2 steady ['stɛdɪ] (a.) 穩定的
3 parcel ['pɑrsl] (n.) 包裹
4 triumphantly [traɪ'ʌmfəntlɪ] (adv.) 得意洋洋地
5 steer [stɪr] (v.) 掌舵；駕駛
6 land [lænd] (v.) 登陸
7 draw [drɔ] (v.) 畫（動詞三態：draw; drew; drawn）

Lily's vision

- What vision has Lily had?

  ☐ A vision of the house, the lawn, the sea and the lighthouse

  ☐ A vision of the meaning of life

  ☐ A vision of mother and child

  ☐ A vision of a moment in time

AFTER READING

Ⓐ Personal Response

1 Who said this? Match the quotes to the characters.

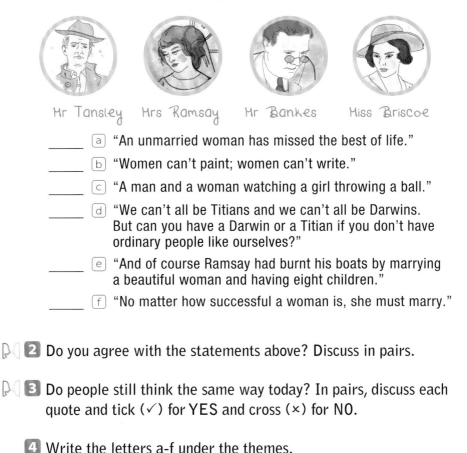

Mr Tansley   Mrs Ramsay   Mr Bankes   Miss Briscoe

_____ ⓐ "An unmarried woman has missed the best of life."

_____ ⓑ "Women can't paint; women can't write."

_____ ⓒ "A man and a woman watching a girl throwing a ball."

_____ ⓓ "We can't all be Titians and we can't all be Darwins. But can you have a Darwin or a Titian if you don't have ordinary people like ourselves?"

_____ ⓔ "And of course Ramsay had burnt his boats by marrying a beautiful woman and having eight children."

_____ ⓕ "No matter how successful a woman is, she must marry."

2 Do you agree with the statements above? Discuss in pairs.

3 Do people still think the same way today? In pairs, discuss each quote and tick (✓) for **YES** and cross (✗) for **NO**.

4 Write the letters a-f under the themes.

Literature and Art	Women and Marriage

B Comprehension

5 Tick true (T) or false (F).

☐T ☐F ⓐ Mr and Mrs Ramsay have ten children.

☐T ☐F ⓑ Mrs Ramsay is one of the greatest philosophers of her age.

☐T ☐F ⓒ Lily Briscoe doesn't want anyone to see her painting.

☐T ☐F ⓓ The children all tease William Bankes.

☐T ☐F ⓔ Charles Tansley has never been to a circus.

☐T ☐F ⓕ Mrs Ramsay is knitting a pair of socks for James.

6 Correct the false sentences.

7 How many of these small details in the novel did you notice? Complete the sentences.

ⓐ Mr Tansley was poor. He often didn't have a _____ in winter.

ⓑ Minta Doyle lost her _____ on the beach.

ⓒ Mr Carmichael shuffled past in a pair of yellow _____.

ⓓ Mr Bankes took out a _____ and tapped Lily's painting with it.

ⓔ The gap in the thick hedge was guarded by _____.

ⓕ Mrs Ramsay used to wear an old gray _____ for gardening.

8 Put these events from the story in the correct order.

_____ a Lily Briscoe finally finished her painting.

_____ b Mrs Ramsay died.

_____ c Mr Ramsay took Cam and James to the lighthouse.

_____ d Paul Rayley proposed to Minta Doyle.

_____ e Mrs Ramsay decided that William Bankes and Lily Briscoe should marry.

_____ f The house lay empty for years.

_____ g Lily Briscoe and Mr Carmichael returned to the house to visit Mr Ramsay and the children.

9 Answer the questions with the name of a character.

Mr Tansley   Miss Briscoe   Mr Ramsay   Mrs Ramsay

_____ a Whose ideas become old-fashioned and outdated?

_____ b Who learns something of the meaning of life?

_____ c Who wanted to carry Mrs Ramsay's bag?

_____ d Whose painting made Lily feel inadequate?

_____ e Who worried that people would stop reading his books?

_____ f Who decided to argue that the man in the lift was more important than Shakespeare?

_____ g Who thought that all the women despised him?

10 In your opinion, which is the most tragic event of the story? Discuss in pairs.

⊙ Characters

11 Which character says this? Do you agree with him/her?

"How then did you judge people?
How did you decide that you liked them or disliked them?"

12 Do you like Mr Ramsay? Write the adjectives in the correct columns.

bad-tempered   self-centered   selfish
dynamic   intelligent

I like Mr Ramsay because he is . . .	I don't like Mr Ramsay because he is . . .

13 Do you like Mrs Ramsay? Write the adjectives in the correct columns.

arrogant   unselfish   domineering   modest
kind   dutiful   generous

I like Mrs Ramsay because she is . . .

I don't like Mrs Ramsay because she is . . .

14 Look through the story and find two more things to add to each column for each character.

15 Match the phrases to the male characters.

Mr Ramsay   Mr Carmichael   Mr Tansley   Mr Bankes

_____ ⓐ He lives for science.

_____ ⓑ He always wants sympathy.

_____ ⓒ He has no charm.

_____ ⓓ His last book was not his best book.

_____ ⓔ He has written a successful book of war poems.

_____ ⓕ They call him the little atheist.

_____ ⓖ He's modest. He doesn't like praise.

_____ ⓗ He translated poetry.

_____ ⓘ He's a widower and he doesn't have any children.

D Plot and Theme

16 There are lots of references to the roles of men and women in society at the time of the novel. Match a sentence from Column A with a quote from Column B.

Column A

Column B

a A man's role in life was much more important than a woman's.

1 (Mrs Ramsay) was afraid, for example, to tell (Mr Ramsay) about the greenhouse roof. "It'll cost fifty pounds to mend it."

b Women were not as educated or intellectual as men.

2 What (Mrs Ramsay) gave the world, in comparison with what (Mr Ramsay) gave, was nothing.

c Women were in charge of running the house and the finances.

3 (William Bankes) had no wife, and no children and he dined alone. In pity for him, (Mrs Ramsay) began the business of conversation.

d Without the support of a wife, a man struggled in life.

4 No matter how successful a woman was (Mrs Ramsay cared nothing for Lily's painting), she must marry.

e Women had no place in society except as a wife.

5 The stupidity of women's minds annoyed (Mr Ramsay).

17 Are the roles of men and women in society still the same today or have things changed? In pairs, discuss.

18 Click T (true) or F (false).

T F ⓐ The characters' thoughts are more important to the plot than the actions.

T F ⓑ Mrs Ramsay's daughters, like their mother, believe in dutifulness and marriage.

T F ⓒ The characters that marry are punished in the novel. They die early or their partners die early or they have unhappy lives.

T F ⓓ Mr Ramsay regrets marrying and having children.

T F ⓔ James and Cam think their father is a bully.

T F ⓕ Happy memories are matches struck in the dark. They give a meaning to life.

19 Time is an important theme in the novel. Answer the questions below.

ⓐ How many pages are there in the first part of the novel, *The Window*?

ⓑ How much time passes?

ⓒ How many pages are there in the second part of the novel, *Time Passes*?

ⓓ How much time passes?

ⓔ How many pages are there in the third part of the novel, *The Lighthouse*?

ⓕ How much time passes?

ⓖ Why do you think the author organizes the story like this? What is she saying about time?

20 How does the story differ from the story you wrote in the *Before Reading* section? In pairs, discuss.

🄴 Language

21 When Lily Briscoe and the Ramsay family finally returned to
the house after the war, what <u>had</u> happened? Complete the
sentences.

- [a] Mrs Ramsay
- [b] Paul Rayley
- [c] Prue
- [d] Andrew
- [e] Charles Tansley
- [f] Mr Carmichael

22 In the opinions of some characters in the book, what *should* or
shouldn't people do? Match the phrases to the people and write
sentences.

be aware that life is difficult
never have married
fight tyranny to the death
marry
fall in love with Mr Tansley
know that Mr Ramsay was much more important than she was
interfere in other people's lives

- [a] People
- [b] Children
- [c] Lily Briscoe
- [d] Mrs Ramsay
- [e] Prue
- [f] Mr Ramsay
- [g] James and Cam

23 Complete the phrases from the novel with the words below.

temper   teeth   boats   date   bullying   death

a He must be bored to _____.

b She had escaped marriage by the skin of her _____.

c He wanted to stamp out _____.

d He often loses his _____.

e She was dusty and out of _____.

f He had burnt all his _____ when he got married and had eight children.

24 Who do the sentences refer to? Write the names next to the sentences.

James   Mrs Ramsay   the Lighthouse keeper
Mr Ramsay   Lily Briscoe

25 Read the sentences below. They create strong images using alliteration. Write a sentence about the lighthouse using alliteration.

A shot went off nearby, and there came, flying from its fragments, a frightened flock of birds.

Following the scatter of swift-flying birds in the sky.

The sigh of all the seas round the islands soothed them.

26 This sentence creates a powerful image. Is there a sentence in the text that creates a strong image for you? In pairs, discuss.

"There was a purplish stain upon the surface of the sea now, as if something had boiled and bled, invisibly, beneath."

TEST

1 Complete the sentences. Circle 1, 2 or 3.

a At the beginning of the novel, James wants to go to the
   1 circus.   2 lighthouse.   3 village.

b Mr Ramsay is afraid that people will stop
   1 looking at his paintings.
   2 reading his books.
   3 attending his lectures.

c Mrs Ramsay wants her daughters
   1 to become successful painters.
   2 to stay single and independent.
   3 to marry and have children.

d William Bankes is envious of Mr Ramsay because he
   1 has children.
   2 has a beautiful wife.
   3 is a great philosopher.

e Sometimes painting makes Lily Briscoe feel
   1 intelligent.
   2 lonely.
   3 inadequate.

f Andrew and Prue experience
   1 loneliness.
   2 an untimely death.
   3 a bad marriage.

2 What did Mrs Ramsay say about the characters? Match the sentence halves.

_____ (a) Prue took

_____ (b) Andrew had

_____ (c) Minta Doyle was

_____ (d) Lily Briscoe had

_____ (e) Mr Ramsay was

_____ (f) William Bankes had

_____ (g) Charles Tansley shouldn't

_____ (h) James was

_____ (i) Mr Carmichael could

(1) the most sensitive of all her children.

(2) a much more important person than she was.

(3) a sad life with no wife and no children.

(4) your breath away with her beauty.

(5) a spark of something she liked, but no man would like.

(6) an extraordinary gift for mathematics.

(7) a tomboy.

(8) have been a great philosopher if he hadn't made a bad marriage.

(9) marry Prue.

3 Talk about the picture. Look at the pictures on pages 20 and 31.

Who are in the pictures?

How are the pictures similar and how are they different?

Describe the mood of each picture.

PROJECT WORK

1 Landscape

a) Search the Internet for the landscape of the Isle of Skye and its lighthouses. Create a collage illustrating how you imagine the view from the Ramsays's house. Then describe the evocative quality of such a setting and how it affects the mood of the people in the novel.

b) Are houses and landscapes influenced by the events of the people who've lived there? Find examples in the novel of the link between the Ramsays' house, the cycle of the seasons and the events in the characters' lives.

c) Which artist would you ask to paint the house, the sea, the lighthouse and the people? Search the Internet for suitable styles. Look up impressionism, pointillism, art nouveau, surrealism and fauvism or look up one of your favorite painters and imagine what they would do with this subject.

Isle of Skye

Carl Gustav Jung and Sigmund Freud

2 People

Family relationships can be complicated and disturbing. Virginia Woolf (1882-1941) doesn't fully develop any of the relationships in the novel, as she is interested in people's thoughts and ideas, not their psyche. Yet she was a contemporary of Carl Gustav Jung (1875-1961) and Sigmund Freud (1856-1939).

Search the Internet to find out when they lived and the theories they developed. Would you apply any of these theories to the characters in the novel?

作者簡介 　維吉尼亞‧吳爾夫於 1882 年 1 月 25 日出生於倫敦，她家境富裕，住家環境優渥。她自幼便在書堆與知性的對話中成長。

　　維吉尼亞有一個不幸的人生，她身邊的許多至親都英年早逝，而她的一生中也經歷過多次的精神崩潰。1904 年父親過世後，她搬到倫敦的布盧姆茨伯里區，在那裡和哥哥及友人共同幫忙成立了「布盧姆茨伯里派」。這是一個由作家和藝術家所組成的文藝團體，對二十世紀初英國的人文觀點造成了很大的影響。

　　1912 年，維吉尼亞與李奧納‧吳爾夫結婚，李奧納穩定的個性正投合了維吉尼亞的需要。

　　維吉尼亞公認是英語語言風格的一位重要革新者，也是現代化運動的一位指標性作家。她所使用的文學技巧稱作「意識流」，藉以表達劇中人物的內心獨白。

　　她共創作了九部小說、兩本傳記、一本短篇小說、五本散文與評論選和一本日記選輯。她最有名的小說包括《達洛維夫人》（Mrs. Dalloway）、《燈塔行》（To the Lighthouse）和《自己的房間》（A Room of One's Own）。

　　1941 年三月，她於東薩塞克斯郡住家附近投河自盡。她在寄給丈夫的信件上寫道，她感覺到自己瀕臨精神錯亂的邊緣，所以她不想拖累他。

李書簡介 　《燈塔行》是維吉尼亞‧吳爾夫最具自傳性的一本小說。她的姊姊凡娜莎‧貝爾（她是畫家，和劇中人物莉莉‧布斯克一樣）在讀此書時，覺得她們的父母躍然紙上。維吉尼亞的丈夫認為這本書是一部傑作。

　　在維吉尼亞十三歲以前，他們全家人每年夏天都會去康沃爾的聖艾維斯避暑別墅避暑。她的母親就像劇中人物朗茲夫人一樣，會邀請倫敦的朋友一起去度假，所以他們的別墅裡總是高朋滿座。在黃昏時刻，他們會遠望著高卓維燈塔的光芒。1895 年，她的母親去世，自此之後，她的父親也和劇中的朗茲先生一樣，不願重返聖艾維斯。

　　這本小說不強調劇情發展，而是透過一系列的內心獨白來鋪陳，主題多圍繞著女性社會角色的自覺，以及死亡與變遷。在維吉尼亞生長的年代中，女性的天職是賢妻良母，社會由男性所主宰，這是正常的社會規範。

　　維吉尼亞反對這種觀點，在她的小說中，接受賢妻良母這種角色的女性會遭到厄運，她們的婚姻會以悲劇或厭膩收場，生產分娩的最終結果往往是死亡，而只有獨立單身的女性能夠倖存下來。

　　家人的死亡帶給維吉尼亞很大的陰影，她希望透過劇中的人物來戰勝死亡。朗茲夫人希望自己死後能被人們所記得，朗茲先生希望死後自己所寫的書還會被人們所閱讀，莉莉‧布斯克希望自己的畫作能為後世的人所欣賞。這些角色都在追求一種永恆，或許作者本身也是這樣吧。

I. 窗

P.15

「當然好啊，如果明天天氣放晴的話。」朗茲夫人説：「只不過你要很早起就是了。」她又補了一句。

這些話讓六歲大的兒子聽了煞是開心，都説定了，這趟旅程轉眼成行。兒子這些年來就盼著這次的出遊，而今只要再過一個黑漆漆的晚上，然後搭上一天的船，旅程就展開了。

詹姆士‧朗茲坐在地板上，歡天喜地地剪著型錄上的圖案。母親看著他整整齊齊地剪下冰箱的圖樣，不禁心想，「他的樣子好認真啊，可以想見他穿上紅袍、戴上白色假髮、當上法官的樣子，甚至可以想見他帶領國家度過危機的樣子。」

「明天的天氣不會變好。」詹姆士的父親在起居室的窗戶前停下腳步，説道。

P.16

這一刻，詹姆士真想殺了父親。朗茲先生就是很會刺激孩子。他站在那裡，身影細如刀鋒。他澆兒子冷水、嘲諷妻子，不禁露出得意的笑容。妻子要比他好上千萬倍（詹姆士這麼覺得）。

朗茲先生知道自己料事如神，他説的事都很靈驗，沒失準過。他從不肯修飾一下自己令人不快的措詞來讓別人高興一下，尤其對自己的孩子更是如此。

「他們應該從小就要知道人生的路不好走。」他心想。

「但天氣也可能會放晴。」朗茲夫人一邊織著棕色襪子，一邊説道。

如果這些襪子能夠趕快織完，那麼等他們真的去燈塔時，她要把襪子交給燈塔員，送給他的小兒子。她還想拿些舊雜誌和菸草給他。房子裡堆放的那些所有用不著的東西，她都想拿去送給他。她就是想送給窮人什麼東西的，好讓他們高興一下。窮人的生活沒有調劑，除了清清油燈，就只能整天枯坐，百無聊賴。

「你們會想待在一個和網球場一樣大的島上，然後被暴風雨困在那裡困上一個月嗎？你們會希望怎麼看都看不到半個人嗎？你們會想日復一日望著一成不變的無聊海浪嗎？你們會想過那樣的生活嗎？」她問女兒們：「所以我們一定要盡可能帶東西過去慰勞他們。」

111

孤獨

- 你比較喜歡獨處，還是比較喜歡有人作伴？
- 想像一下燈塔員的生活，和夥伴分享彼此的想法。

「現在在刮正西風。」無神論的湯司禮說道。

正西風剛好是最不適合登陸燈塔的風向。

他哪壺不開提哪壺，朗茲夫人心想。這讓詹姆士更失望了。不過朗茲夫人不准孩子們譏笑湯司禮。孩子們都叫他是「小無神論者」，蘿絲取笑他，苦露取笑他，安德魯、賈斯柏和羅傑也取笑他。

朗茲夫人討厭怠慢客人，尤其是怠慢年輕的男客人。她邀請了很多才華洋溢的窮小子在假日時跟他們一起去天空島度假。沒錯，她是所有男性的庇護者，男士們殷勤有禮，而且渾身是膽，他們還跟別的國家訂定了條約，統治了印度，掌控了經濟。

她攬鏡自照，看到年屆半百的自己已經髮絲斑白，她想，「我應該把生活打理得更好才對──包括丈夫、金錢，和丈夫創作的書。不過我是從不後悔當初做了結婚的決定。」

她不是一個可以敷衍的女性，苦露、南希和蘿絲這些女兒們只能趁著安靜的時刻，想像一下另一種不同於母親的生活，例如像是巴黎的生活。那是一種可以奔放的生活，不用老是想著要去呵護男性。女兒們都默默質疑著母親對責任與婚姻的價值觀，那是對「天職」、「婚姻」和「美」的一種內心質疑。

「你們明天去不了燈塔了。」查爾斯·湯司禮和她丈夫一起站在窗戶前，他一邊拍著手，一邊說道。他的發言顯然是夠多了。

「真希望他們兩個人趕快離開，不要在這裡打擾我和詹姆士。」她一邊盯著湯司禮看，一邊想，「用孩子們的話來說，他真是一個悲哀的男人。他不會打板球，走起路來都是用拖的，而且講話酸溜溜的。他最喜歡做的事，就是在朗茲先生的身邊跟前跟後，然後嘴裡唸著誰得了什麼什麼獎，誰的拉丁詩寫得最好，誰是貝列爾學院的超級天才。他們就聊這些。」

朗茲夫人站在起居室的窗前，此時浮現在她心頭的是貧富問題，還有她在這裡以及在倫敦所親眼目睹的一些事情。她探問過這位寡婦，拜訪過那位辛苦謀生的妻子。她在一本筆記本上，用鉛筆寫下所得和支出，記錄上工下崗的情況。這是一個無法解決的問題。

湯司禮先生尾隨她走進起居室，然後站在桌子旁邊。人都走光了──孩子們、蜜塔·朵伊、保羅·瑞雷、奧古司·卡邁可，還有她的丈夫，他們都離開了。

她轉過身，嘆口氣說：「湯司禮先生，你要跟我一起出門嗎？我要去街上辦些雜事，我有一、兩封信要寫。你等我十分鐘,我去戴頂帽子。」

十分鐘後,就看到她提著籃子、拿著陽傘回來,準備就緒。

她途中停了一會兒,詢問卡邁可先生要不要幫他帶些什麼回來。卡邁可先生當時正在打盹,一雙像貓一樣的褐黃色眼睛半睜半寐。就像貓眼那樣,他的眼底映出搖曳的樹影和飄浮而過的雲朵,眼裡沒有流露出任何的思緒。

P.21

「我們要出征囉,」她笑著説:「我們要去街上一趟,你需要郵票、文件紙還是菸草嗎?」她問道。

不需要,卡邁可先生什麼也不需要。

「他早應該成為一個大哲學家的,」他們走在通往漁村的路上時,朗茲夫人説:「只可惜他娶錯了老婆。」

她撐著黑色洋傘,把他的往事説了出來。他在牛津邂逅了一位女孩,兩人年紀輕輕就結了婚。他們沒什麼錢,後來去了印度,他在那裡翻譯小品詩,「我想那些詩一定很美」。這時他們看到他正往草地上躺下去。

朗茲夫人講出這些事情,讓查爾斯‧湯司禮覺得是對自己的一種禮遇。他感覺好多了。她崇尚男性的才智,認為凡是當妻子的都應該以丈夫的工作為重。她並非是在怪罪女方,她相信他們的婚姻過得很美滿。

朗茲夫人讓湯司禮感到自己受到了尊重。如果他們現在搭馬車,他會很樂意付車費。至於她的小籃子,他應該幫忙拿嗎?

不用勞煩他了,她回答。她這個籃子

都是自己提的,的確是這樣沒錯,他感覺得出來。他感覺到許多事情,而且有些事情特別讓他感到既興奮又困擾。

P.23

他想讓她看看自己穿著大學教授服、走在行列裡的樣子,堂堂一個教授職位——但她現在在看的是什麼?她注視著一個正在張貼海報的男人。刷子每刷一下,就可以看到海報上露出更多的腿、鐵環和馬匹,畫面是亮紅色和藍色的,直到馬戲團海報鋪滿了半面牆。

「上百位騎師,二十隻會耍馬戲的海豹、獅子、老虎……即將蒞臨本地,」她讀著海報,説道,「我們大家都一起來看吧!」她童心未泯地開心叫道。

「我們走吧。」他故意重覆用她説過的語法來回答,讓她覺得不舒服。

是什麼事情讓他講話不得體、感覺不對勁了?她不明白。他是怎麼了嗎?這一刻,她對他產生了憐憫之情。

113

「你小的時候，沒有人帶你去看過馬戲團嗎？」她問。

「沒有。」他回答。

他來自一大口子的家庭，家中有九個兄弟姊妹，父親是勞動分子。

「朗茲夫人，我父親是一位藥師，他開了一家藥鋪，我從十三歲就開始掙錢養自己了。」

冬天時，他常常沒有大衣可以穿。他都抽最便宜的菸草，而且工作要很拼。

P.25

他們繼續走著，朗茲夫人聽著他描述，卻不太能夠體會，她只能聽懂一些字眼，像是論文、研究員、高級講師、大學講師。

她暗忖道：「我一定不准孩子們再譏笑他了，這個可憐的年輕人。」

他們這時已經來到鎮上的大馬路上。他們一路上聊著天，談到了教學、勞動分子和講課的事情。當他們走出鎮上、往碼頭走去時，他打算開口跟她講一些事。

整個海灣在他們眼前展開，朗茲夫人不禁興奮地喊道：「哇，好美啊！」

一片湛藍的海水橫在眼前，遠處的海水中矗立著一個高高的燈塔，往燈塔的右方望去，可以遠望到綠色的沙丘，上面長滿了野生的雜草。

「我先生就喜歡這樣的景色。」她說完，便閉上了嘴。

湯司禮先生這時產生了一股強烈的情緒。這股情緒從他剛才在花園想幫她提籃子時就開始醞釀。到了鎮上，當他想向她傾訴自己的所有事情時，情緒變得更加波動。這實在太不尋常了。

P.26

他跟她來到一間小屋子裡。她上樓去探望一位婦女，他便站在客廳裡等候她。他能聽得到她講話的聲音，他迫不及待想再陪她一路走回家，並且幫她提籃子。

這時，他聽到她走出房間、關上房門的聲音，聽到她說：「妳要讓窗戶開著，門都要關好，房子裡缺什麼都要講。」

突然，就在她走進客廳時，他頓時明白了，原來她是他所見過最美麗的人。

她的眸子裡閃著星光，風兒在她的髮絲間流動──他在想什麼蠢事啊！她都已經年過半百、生過八個孩子啦！他們走過花草地，星星在她眸子裡閃爍，微風在她的髮絲間吹拂。他幫她提了籃子。

「再見了，愛兒希。」她說完，兩人便往街上走去。

一個正在挖排水道的工人停下來注視她，這讓查爾斯·湯司禮有生以來第一次感到這麼神氣。他正和一位美麗的女士偕伴而行，而且他還幫她提籃子。

P. 27

「詹姆士，你去不了燈塔了。」湯司禮先生説。

「真是一個惹人厭的年輕人，為什麼老是提這件事？」朗茲夫人心想。

「也許我們明天醒來，會看到陽光普照，聽到小鳥啾啾叫。」她一邊把詹姆士的頭髮撥平，一邊慈祥地説道。

詹姆士是那麼想去看燈塔。

這時她聽到講話聲沉寂下來。沒有人在説話。她聆聽著，之後聽到了花園裡傳來了一個充滿節奏的聲音，像是歌唱聲，又像是講話聲。這時，突然迸出一個叫喊聲：

槍林彈雨，傾天而下！

她緊張地轉過身，瞧瞧是否有人聽到丈夫的聲音。她很高興她只看到了莉莉·布斯克。這沒事的。不過看到莉莉站在草坪邊寫生，她才想到自己的頭應該保持同一個姿勢，讓莉莉好好畫她。莉莉的畫作！朗茲夫人笑了笑。

「她的眼睛長得像中國人的小眼睛，臉色又那麼蒼白，應該是嫁不出去了。」她想。

P. 28

不能用太嚴肅的態度來看莉莉的繪畫，她是一個獨立的小婦人，朗茲夫人就喜歡她這一點。所以啦，她把頭彎下來，這是説好了的姿勢。

朗茲先生這時揮著手朝她的方向跑過來，差點撞倒了莉莉的畫架。只聽他大聲喊道：

我們無畏地策馬湧來！

謝天謝地，他一個掉頭，策馬走開了，準備在巴拉鎮英勇犧牲，莉莉這樣猜想著。

115

他是一個會讓人生畏、又讓人覺得好笑的人，不過只要他像這樣揮手叫喊，就表示她很安全。

「他不會停下來看我的畫，」她鬆了一口氣，心想。「我不想讓別人看到我的畫。」

想像

· 想像一下畫面，發生了什麼事？從下面三組句子中，勾選出正確的句子，然後閉上眼睛，想像那些畫面。

☐ 朗茲夫人和莉莉在屋子裡。
☐ 朗茲夫人和莉莉在花園裡。
☐ 莉莉在畫朗茲夫人的肖畫像。
☐ 莉莉在和朗茲夫人講話。
☐ 朗茲先生一路叫喊著跑過草坪。
☐ 朗茲先生佇足下來看繪畫。

P.29

然而，這時走來了其他的人。聽這個腳步聲，應該是威廉·班克斯。但她並沒有把畫轉向草坪。如果換成是別人，她會把畫轉過去。

他們兩個人現在都住在村子裡，會一起走進走出，聊聊湯品，聊聊孩子們，天南地北地聊，兩人於是成了好朋友。這時，他來到她的身邊，她就站在原地不動。（他的年紀大到可以當她父親，他是一位植物學家，妻子已經過世。他身上散發出整潔清新的香皂味道。）

因為和她待在同一個屋簷下，他注意到她很有規律，一定會在早餐之前起床，然後出外寫生。她沒有錢，外表也不如朵伊小姐，不過她很敏銳，眼神也比朵伊小姐慧黠。譬如，像朗茲先生此

時這樣一邊叫喊、一邊揮手而來的行逕，布斯克小姐就能讀得懂。

有人下錯指令釀禍了！

P.30

朗茲先生用很兇的眼神看了他們一眼，讓他們倆錯愕了一下，他們都不是故意要撞見這一幕的。

班克斯先生於是趕緊說：天氣變冷了。他提議兩個人一起去散個步。她同意了，不過要她停下畫筆是需要一點掙扎的。

她很喜歡畫畫，可是一拿起畫筆，又會覺得自己畫得不夠好。她把畫筆整整齊齊地放進畫箱裡，然後對威廉·班克斯說：「沒錯，天氣變冷了。」

畢竟現在已經九月中了，而且已經過了傍晚六點了。

他們住花園裡走去，途中經過網球場的草坪，穿過一片高草地，來到濃密樹籬間的一處空地，旁邊是一片劍葉蘭。從劍葉蘭這邊望過去，海灣的藍色海水被烘托得更加湛藍了。

他們每天傍晚都會來這裡。他們站在那裡，兩人笑容洋溢，內心裡感到很滿足。

望著沙丘，威廉·班克斯想到了朗茲，想到了西莫連的一條馬路，想到當時朗茲就走在那條馬路上，走在他的前方。他想，他們的友誼，就是在那條馬路上走到了盡頭。

之後，朗茲結婚了。從那時候起，他們的友誼就變質了。不過，他說他還是很欽佩和尊敬朗茲。

P. 32

他從眼前的景色中別過頭去。他們開始沿著車道走回房子。他們看到了卡梅，她是朗茲的么女，正在採著花朵。她個性刁蠻，不可能「為紳士獻花」，因為這是奶媽告誡她的。不，絕對不可能！她跺著腳，讓班克斯先生覺得自己又老又可悲。

朗茲家並不寬裕，他們有八個孩子要養！誰有本事靠著哲學來養活八個小孩？上學要錢（朗茲夫人自己大概有一點錢，沒錯），衣服也要錢。

價值觀

- 就你來看，你覺得什麼比較重要？勾選以下的項目。
  - ☐ 婚姻幸福
  - ☐ 事業有成
  - ☐ 教育小孩
  - ☐ 交友

P. 33

他們沿著車道走回來，對於他的發言，莉莉・布斯克一路上只回答「是」與「不是」。他提到了朗茲，他一方面為他感到惋惜，一方面卻也羨慕他。

孩子們為朗茲帶來了很不一樣的東西，威廉・班克斯能看出這一點。他希望卡梅會在他的外套上插一朵花，或是爬上他的肩膀，就好像她對待她的父親那樣。

不過，孩子們也會毀掉一些東西，他的老友們作如是想。那莉莉・布斯克是怎麼想的？令人意外的是，像他一個這麼聰明的人，竟然會那麼依賴別人的讚美。

「哦，但是你想想他的著作！」莉莉說。

她只要「一想到他的著作」，眼前就浮現一個大廚房桌。這都要怪安德魯。

她問他說：「你父親的書都寫些什麼？」

「主體、客體和實相。」安德魯回答。

她說她聽得不是很懂。

「那你就想像一下，你不在廚房裡時，廚房的桌子是什麼樣子的。」安德魯回答她。

從此，她只要一想到朗茲先生的著作，腦海裡就會浮現出廚房的桌子。

P. 34

她說「想想他的著作」，這話深得威廉・班克斯的心。他自己也常在思索這件事。他說了好幾次：「有些人最好的作品會在四十歲以前問世，朗茲便是屬於這樣的人。」

他在年僅二十五歲時出版的那本書薄薄的書，對哲學界做出了一定的貢獻。他之後的著作，就多多少少是炒冷飯。

這一刻，莉莉·布斯克對班克斯先生油然生起了景仰之情。你不會自我炫耀，你比朗茲先生出色，你是我所見過最優秀的人類。你沒有妻小的家累，你為科學而活。如果說要讚美你，對你反而是一種侮辱。你心懷仁慈，寬宏大量，是一個真正的勇者！

不過接著，她想起了他來蘇格蘭一路上帶著的貼身男僕。男僕不喜歡狗坐在椅子上。他用了幾個鐘頭來談蔬菜裡的鹽分、批評英國的廚師。那你是如何來對別人下評論的？你是怎麼決定喜不喜歡他們的？

她佇足望著洋梨樹，琢磨著這兩個男人。要跟上她的思緒，就好比要速記一個講話飛快的人一樣，來不及抄寫，更何況她心裡頭的聲音是充滿了矛盾。

P.35

朗茲先生自私又自大，囂張又跋扈，讓朗茲夫人疲於奔命。不過，他卻擁有你所沒有的（她在心裡這樣對班克斯先生講）。他生氣蓬勃，不會管那些瑣事，而且他喜歡狗、喜歡自己的孩子。他生了八個孩子，而班克斯膝下無子。

這些聲音在莉莉的腦海裡此起彼落。這時，附近響起了一聲槍響，一群受到驚嚇的野雁七零八落地驚慌飛過。

「是賈斯柏！」班克斯先生說。

他們轉身望著鳥群高高飛過露臺。他們追隨著急亂飛過天空的四散鳥群，穿

過樹籬間的空地，撞見了朗茲先生。朗茲先生激動地對著他們大聲喊道：

有人下錯指令釀禍了！

P.37

朗茲先生看了莉莉和班克斯先生一眼，就在準備理睬他們時，卻又很快轉身離開。

莉莉·布斯克和班克斯先生緊張地抬頭望向天空，看著賈斯柏用槍射擊的鳥群，鳥群正棲息在樹梢上。

「就算明天不會放晴，」朗茲夫人看著一旁走過的莉莉·布斯克和威廉·班克斯，說道：「總有一天也會放晴。現在……」她一邊說，一邊想著：莉莉的中國小眼睛和蒼白的膚色，正是她獨有的味道，聰明的男人才會懂得欣賞。「現在站起來，讓我量量你的腳。我們有可能會去燈塔，讓我看一下襪子是不是夠長。」

她突然靈機一動，不禁笑了笑。威廉和莉莉應該湊成一對。她拿起襪子，對著詹姆士的腳比了比。

接著，她抬起頭，看看房間，看看椅子，覺得椅子太舊了。但是，買好一點的椅子又有什麼用？到了濕冷的冬天，椅子還是會壞得很快。不過，沒關係！租金才兩個半便士，而且孩子們很喜歡。這對丈夫來說也未嘗不好，可以讓他離開書房和教室三千里遠，講準確一點，是三百里遠；而且這裡有客房。

P.39

「親愛的，站好。」她對詹姆士說。她想，「很快的，房子就會舊到需要整修了。」

如果她能教會孩子們要把腳踩乾淨，不要把海邊的沙子帶進門，情況會好一點。每經過一個夏天，屋子裡的東西就愈來愈陳舊。腳踏墊褪色了，壁紙也褪色了，早看不出上面的玫瑰圖樣了。

她一陣心煩，便不假辭色地對詹姆士說：「站好。」

襪子短了半吋左右。

「太短了，」她說：「差太多了。」

朗茲夫人一邊織著棕色襪子，一邊在小兒子的額頭上親吻了一下。

「去找別的圖樣來剪吧。」她說。

有人下錯指令釀禍了！

朗茲夫人抬頭看。

有人下錯指令釀禍了！

P.40

她抬頭看丈夫，丈夫正朝著她走過來。看來有事情發生了，有人捅了漏子，只是她不知道是怎麼一回事。

朗茲先生打著哆嗦。「槍林彈雨，傾天而下。我們無畏地策馬湧來，通過了死亡谷，和莉莉·布斯克和威廉·班克斯正面交鋒」。他渾身顫抖著。

朗茲夫人沒和他說話。按這些熟悉的跡象來判斷，他現在很煩躁。她拍拍詹姆士的頭，把她對丈夫的感覺轉移到兒子身上。她看到他正在將型錄上的一件白色襯衫塗上黃色。

她想，他要是能夠成為一位大藝術家，那她會很高興的。怎就不能呢？

接著，丈夫又從旁邊走過，她抬頭看了看。她看到他冷靜了下來，不禁鬆了口氣。

家庭生活還是居了上風。他在窗前停下腳步，彎下腰用手指在詹姆士裸露的腿上搔了搔癢。詹姆士把他的手撥開，

119

覺得父親很討厭。

「我打算趕緊把這些襪子織完，明天好拿去給燈塔看守員的小兒子。」朗茲夫人說。

「你們明天去不了燈塔的。」朗茲先生沒好氣地說。

「你怎麼就知道？風向說變就變」她說。

女性的不明事理惱怒了他，他在石階上跺了一下腳。

P.41

「真是的。」他說。

而她怎麼回應呢？她只說明天可能會放晴，所以有可能成行。

「如果氣溫下降，而且又吹正西風，那就別想了。」他說。

「他對別人的感受一點同理心也沒有。」她想。

她低下頭，不再說話。沒有什麼需要說的話。

他安靜地站在她旁邊，隨後換了謙遜的口吻說道：「如果你想的話，我可以去問海巡員。」

「我想你說的也對。」她說。

她最敬佩的人就是他了。她覺得自己還不配幫他繫鞋帶。

朗茲先生對自己的壞脾氣感到難為情，他很不好意思地又搔了搔兒子裸露的腿，然後才又出門走進暮色中。

「有人下錯指令釀禍了！」他一邊在露台上來回走來走去，一邊重覆道。不過他這時候的口氣已經改變了，他講「有人下錯指令釀禍了！」的語氣聽起來很滑稽，沒什麼逼真感，讓朗茲夫人不禁莞爾。他來回踱步，沒多久就哼起

歌來，之後便安靜了下來。

P.43

他安全無恙。他停下腳步點煙斗，對著窗戶裡的妻子和兒子又看了看，這一幕能讓他堅強起來，並且感到滿足。不過兒子討厭他，討厭他老是來騷擾他們。

他們正在看童話故事書。他盯著書本的頁面，想要父親自動離開。他用手指著書上的一個字，想讓母親把注意力從父親那裡轉移到他身上，結果沒有奏效，朗茲先生並沒有走開。他站在那裡，想要一點關愛。

他需要一點關愛，朗茲夫人早有了準備。

「他一事無成。」他說。

她幫他說了話。「查爾斯‧湯司禮認為你是當今最傑出的哲學家。」她說。

但這話還不夠滿足他，他需要的是關愛。他想要確定的是，不只這裡需要他，全世界也都需要他。

她手上的棒針閃閃發亮。她挺著背，懷著自信，讓房間充滿了溫暖與光明。她要他自己一個人屋裡屋外到處走走，好好放鬆一下。

她一邊做著女紅，一邊笑了笑。詹姆士站在她的兩膝之間，他覺得父親需要別人的關愛，把母親的精力都耗盡了。

「他一事無成。」他又說了一遍。

P.44

棒針閃閃發亮，她用她的笑容、沉著和能耐來撫慰他。如果他能夠對她有絕對的信心，那就沒有什麼足以傷害他。他耳裡充滿了她的話語，這讓他感覺好

多了。他用感激的眼神看著她，説道：「我去走走，看看孩子們玩板球。」他説完後便離開。

就像花瓣一瓣瓣接連閉合起來那樣，朗茲夫人霎時躬起了身子。她著實累壞了。

當她轉頭回到童話書上時，她生起了一些難忍的感覺。「覺得自己比丈夫優秀」的這種感覺，讓她感到厭惡，一刻都不能忍受。她不希望別人看到他在她的面前是這個樣子的，那樣別人會説他太依賴她了。人們要知道，他比她重要多了。她所能給予這個世界的，和丈夫對這個世界所做的貢獻比起來，根本不足掛齒。

還有一些事情的真相她是不能跟他説的。像是，她不敢告訴他溫室屋頂的事。「這個修理起來要五十英鎊。」還有，他寫的書，她怕他會以為她在想：他最新出版的書，並不是他最好的書（這是她從威廉·班克斯那裡聽來的）。像這樣的事情都會傷害他們婚姻中的喜悦之情、純然的喜悦之情。

書本的頁面上投下了一個影子，她抬頭看了一下，是奧古司·卡邁可。他穿著他的黃色拖鞋，正拖著腳步走過。

「你要進去嗎？」她喊道。

P. 45

他沒有回答。她知道這個可憐的男人很鬱悶。他每年都會過來跟他們一起待著，但這其實是一種逃離。不過，他每年給她的感覺都還是一樣，他並不信任她，這都要怪他老婆。

她回憶起在聖約翰林那個恐怖的小房間裡，當時她親眼目睹了那位苛刻的女人將他轟出門。他很邋遢，會把東西丟在外套上面，是一個在這個世界上無所事事的老男人，於是她就把他趕出家門了。

她用她苛刻的方式説：「朗茲夫人和我現在要小聊一下。」朗茲夫人看出了他生命中諸多悲慘的事情。他有足夠的錢買菸草嗎？他是不是得跟妻子討錢？噢，她不忍心去想像他的妻子是如何地羞辱他。所以現在，他都盡量避開她。

訪客

· 你記得朗茲夫人的訪客的名字嗎？

1. 小無神論者：查爾斯·湯司禮

2. 他早應該成為一個大哲學家的，只可惜他娶錯了老婆：奧古司·卡邁可

3. 一個獨立的小婦人：莉莉·布斯克

4. 丈夫的一位昔日好友，至今仍欽佩、尊重丈夫：威廉·班克斯

P. 46

有什麼是她還能做的？她已經給他一個有日照的房間，而且孩子們對他也很友善。她特別努力地去善待他。她的人緣一向很好，人們也會向她吐露祕密。她拿著「美貌」這把火炬，照亮每一個步入的房間裡。

為了敏感的兒子詹姆士，她應該趕快把《漁夫與妻子》這個故事讀完（她其他的孩子都不像他這麼敏感）。

朗茲夫人希望丈夫不會選這個時候來打斷他們，他為什麼不去看孩子們玩板球？不過他並沒有開口說話，他只是看一看，點點頭，然後走進花園。

他在《時代》中讀到一篇文章，裡頭提到每年去莎士比亞故居參觀的美國觀光客人數。

他自問：「如果莎士比亞沒有出生，今天的世界會有所不一樣嗎？文明是靠偉人來推動的嗎？現在一般人的生活，會過得比法老王時代來得好嗎？」「這可不一定，搞不好最好的狀態是需要有奴隸階級的存在。倫敦地鐵的電梯操作員是不可少的，這個世界因著一般人而存在。」他想。「藝術，不過是人類極致生活中的一種裝飾品。莎士比亞不一定非得存在不可。」

P. 47

他不清楚自己為什麼要評論莎士比亞，然後讚揚站在電梯門口的人員。他答應了六個星期之後要在卡地夫大學向學生談談洛克、休姆和貝克萊，還有法國大革命爆發的原因。他想以上這些都會在講題中提到。

他走向莉莉和班克斯先生，然後停下腳步，靜靜地站在那裡望著大海。這時，他又轉身走開。

「沒錯。」班克斯先生看著他走開，說道：「只可惜朗茲的行為舉止無法稍微像一般人那樣正常一點。」（因為他喜歡莉莉·布斯克，所以跟她討論了朗茲這個人。）

「我喜歡朗茲先生是因為我想到，他的小指頭要是傷了一下，天就會塌下來。」她說。「我不喜歡他的是他的小心眼，還有他很鈍。」她說。

「他有一點點偽君子嗎？」班克斯先生望著朗茲先生的背影問道。

他想起他的友誼，想到卡梅不肯把花拿給他，想到那些男孩們、女孩們，他還想到自己的住處，他的住處很舒適，但是在妻子過世之後就變得很冷清。當然，他有自己的事業……他還是希望莉莉能夠認同朗茲「有一點點偽君子」的講法。

P. 48

莉莉·布斯克放下畫筆，然後抬頭望望、低頭看看。她抬頭時看到了朗茲先生，他正朝著他們走過來。

「有一點點偽君子嗎？」她重覆了這句話，「噢，他不會，他是最誠懇、最實在（他在這裡是這樣沒錯）、最好的人了。」

不過等她低下頭時，她又想，「他很自我，很跋扈，做人不是很公正。」

班克斯先生期待她回答。當她看到班克斯先生用仰慕的神情望著朗茲夫人時，她便準備開口說些朗茲夫人的不是。不過他那種愛慕的神情，又讓莉莉·布斯克一時忘了自己要說什麼。不過也不是什麼重要的事情，不過就是朗茲夫人個人的一些事情。

「就讓他去看吧，我看我自己的畫就好。」

她很想哭。畫得不好！畫得很不好！

「我不想讓別人看到我的畫，我絕對不會把畫掛起來。」她心想。

湯司禮先生在她的耳邊附耳說過：「女人不會畫畫，女人不會寫作⋯⋯」

這時，她想起來自己想說朗茲夫人的什麼是非了。前幾天晚上，她的高傲之姿激怒了她。她是絕世大美女沒錯，只是太盛氣凌人了。她老是高唱著人一定要有婚姻的歸屬，女人再厲害（朗茲夫人並不把莉莉的畫放在眼裡）也一定要結婚。

「女人不結婚，就會錯過生命中最美好的部分。」她老是這樣說。

P. 49

「噢，但是，我有父親，我有自己的家，而且（她不敢真的把這一點說出來）我也有自己的繪畫作品。」莉莉說。

不過她提的這些理由都微不足道。她喜歡獨處，她不是為婚姻而生的人，只是朗茲夫人一味地認定，親愛的莉莉是個傻女孩。

莉莉轉頭看看班克斯先生，他這時已經戴上眼鏡。他把身子往後挪一步，舉起手，微微地瞇起他清澈的藍色眼睛。

像狗看到有人舉手要打牠一樣，這個動作莉莉讓退縮了一下。她想把畫紙從畫架上撤下，但她沒有這樣做。她已經做好心理準備，等著別人對著自己的作

品品頭論足。如果她的畫一定要給別人看過，那麼班克斯先生就是最佳的人選了。

班克斯先生拿出一把小刀，用刀柄在畫作上輕輕敲了敲。

「你那個地方用紫色的陰影是想呈現什麼？」他問。

「那是朗茲夫人在唸書給詹姆士聽的樣子。」她說。

她知道他指的什麼東西——沒有人能看得出來那是人的身影。

「但我不想畫出具體的樣子。」她說。

「那你為什麼又要把他們畫進作品裡？」他問。

P. 50

繪畫

•莉莉在畫什麼？
☐ 朗茲一家人的肖畫像
☐ 眼前所見的景色
☐ 母親與兒子的肖像

123

P.51

他説得沒錯，為什麼？——是因為那裡的那個角落比較亮，所以這裡的這一塊就應該讓它暗一點。她的畫簡單、清楚、主題很一般，讓班克斯先生看得興味盎然。

「母與子」——這是一個普世都敬重的主題，而在這張畫裡頭，這位母親是一位出了名的美人——可以被簡化成一個紫色的陰影。

他看得很有興致。總算是有人看過她的畫了，而且是一個和她心有靈犀的人。她為此感謝朗茲先生，感謝朗茲夫人，感謝這個時刻、這個地點。她再也不是孤獨一人了。現在，他能夠和別人手挽手地走在長長的藝廊走道上，這真是世界上最奇妙的感覺。

她闔上畫箱，把眼前的畫面永遠地烙印在心裡：畫箱、草坪、班克斯先生，還有在一旁奔跑而過的野女孩卡梅。

卡梅從旁邊跑過去時，敲了一下畫架。她不會為班克斯先生和莉莉·布斯克停下腳步，不會為父親停下腳步，連叫喊著「卡梅，你過來一下！」的母親也是。

她奔跑而過，像隻小鳥，像顆子彈，像支箭。不過只要朗茲夫人再喊一次「卡梅！」，那她就會停下腳步，跑向母親。

P.52

朗茲夫人得重覆問兩次：「安德魯、朵伊小姐和瑞雷先生回來了嗎？」卡梅才會回答説：「還沒，他們還沒回來。」

「蜜塔·朵伊和保羅·瑞雷還沒回來，這只有一種可能性，」朗茲夫人想，「蜜塔已經決定嫁給保羅·瑞雷了！這就對了！」

保羅並不特別出色，但朗茲夫人又想到，她比較喜歡平凡的男人，而不是會寫論文的聰明男人，例如像查爾斯·湯司禮。「他現在一定已經開口求過婚了吧。」

她在這裡幫蜜塔·朵伊和保羅·瑞雷牽姻緣。她為什麼老要説人一定要結婚、生小孩？莫非這是她逃離的一種方式？

「我這樣説有錯嗎？」她自問道，「蜜塔才二十四歲，婚姻需要具備各種條件，她都具備了嗎？現在有下落了嗎？」朗茲夫人想知道。「他們什麼時候會向我報喜？」她是要對蜜塔的父母負責的。「天啊，天啊，他們怎麼會生出這麼男孩子氣的蜜塔？」她自問。

P.53

當然啦，她之前找蜜塔一起吃午餐、喝下午茶、用晚餐，最後讓她跟他們一起來芬萊。蜜塔和她母親還因為這件事而鬧得不愉快。有一個婦女說她「搶了別人家女兒的心」，還說她很強勢，喜歡干涉別人——別人這樣說她，她覺得很不公平。她並不是一個專橫跋扈的人，她更關心的是醫院、排水管和乳品農場，而不是別人家的孩子。

整座島上都沒有醫院，當牛奶送到家門口時都已經髒了。這種事是不合法的。

「這裡再過去有一家模範乳品農場和一家醫院——我想把它們結合起來，但要怎麼做才好呢？我還有這麼多的孩子要照顧，等他們長大一點都上學了，到時候我可能就有時間了。」

噢，她壓根就不希望詹姆士長大，卡梅也是。她希望這兩個孩子能夠永遠保持現在這個樣子，既像個惡魔、又像個天使，帶來厄運，也帶來喜悅。在她的孩子當中，就屬詹姆士最有天賦、個性最敏感了。不過其他的孩子也都前途無量，她是這麼想的。

P.54

菩露美得令人屏息；安德魯，他的數學頭腦連他父親都嘖嘖稱奇；南西和羅傑，他們現在是正野的時候，整天都在球場上玩；至於蘿絲，她的嘴巴長得太大，但是她的手藝很巧，而且不會像賈斯柏那樣喜歡獵鳥；不過喜歡獵鳥只是一個階段罷了。他們都在經歷成長的階段。

她把下巴靠在詹姆士的頭上。他們為什麼要長得這麼快呢？為什麼非得要去上學不可呢？她想要永遠有個小寶寶，懷裡能夠抱著寶寶，就有子萬事足了。她在詹姆士的額前親吻了一下，她想，「這時他人生最快樂的階段了。」接著，她又想起她的這段發言曾經讓丈夫心煩。「我這樣說是沒錯的，他們長大以後就不可能像現在這樣無憂無慮了。」

一份十便士的下午茶，可以讓卡梅高興好幾天。當她走上樓跟孩子們道晚安時，孩子們都正在為自己在花園或海灘上找到的小寶物興奮不已——像是一隻螃蟹，或是一塊石頭。

於是有一晚，她走下樓跟丈夫說：「孩子們為什麼一定要長大呢？他們長大後就不可能像現在這樣快樂了。」

她的話讓他聽了很生氣。「你為什麼

要把人生看得這樣毫無希望？」他說。這種看法是有點怪，但她覺得真正的人生就是這個樣子。他是比她快樂、比她樂觀沒錯，這大概是因為他有工作的關係吧。

P.56

暮色逐漸低垂，她心裡頭擔心著一件事，一時卻忘了是什麼事。之後，她這才想起來，保羅、蜜塔和安德魯都還沒回來。她回想起露台上那一小群準備出門的人。

安德魯帶著他的捕魚網和籃子，準備去抓螃蟹之類的東西。他會爬上岩石，然後被困在岩石上，或是抄斷崖的那些小路走回來，那些小路有可能會崩坍。天都要黑了。

她讀故事書給詹姆士聽，故事已經到了尾聲。「故事結束了。」她說。

接著，她朝海灣望過去，看到燈塔的燈光灑落在海浪上。塔燈已經打開，詹姆士也望著塔燈。

「他終究會問我，『我們要去燈塔那裡了嗎？』這時候我一定要回答，『明天不行，你父親說不行。』」

還好，這時蜜德莉走了進來，準備抱走詹姆士。

蜜德莉抱著他離開時，他還一直轉過頭、望著身後。她知道他在想什麼，「我們明天不會去燈塔那裡。」她心想，「這件事，會一輩子留在他心裡頭。」

他是不會忘記的，她一邊想著，一邊看著他剪下來的圖——一台冰箱，一架除草機，一位穿著禮服的紳士——孩子是不會遺忘事情的。

P.58

孩子

- 你同意「孩子不會遺忘事情」的說法嗎？寫下你以下的兒時記憶：
  - ☐ 你的一次遠足
  - ☐ 一個你曾經遇過的人
  - ☐ 一個很特別的時刻

也因為這樣，大人的言行就變得很重要，等孩子們都上床了，才有機會放鬆。這時候她才可以想怎樣就怎樣，不用去考慮別人。

她望著燈塔規律移動的長長光束，三道光的最後一道光，是她的光，能夠讓她再度平靜下來。

她又開始編織起來。「怎麼有神能創造出這樣一個世界？」她問。「這個世界沒有理性，沒有秩序，沒有正義，

126

只有苦難、死亡和貧窮，沒有永遠的幸福。」這她知道。

丈夫從她身旁走過，留意到了她嚴肅的神情。他不喜歡這樣，這會讓他覺得自己沒有能力保護她。當他走到樹籬那邊時，不禁感到難過。他幫不上什麼忙，事實上，他只會讓情況變得更加嚴重而已。他脾氣不好，對要去燈塔的事感到不耐煩。他對著黑漆漆的樹籬凝視著。

P.59

接著，他又轉過頭來看她。啊，她真是漂亮，而且他覺得她此刻看起來又比以前都漂亮。詹姆士不在，終於只剩下她一個人了，他此時很想過去和她講講話，不過他覺得還是不要比較好。他不能去打擾她。

他靜靜地從她身邊走過。她的樣子這麼憂傷而疏離，令人難以接近，讓他覺得很心疼。他對她愛莫能助。他再度從她身旁走過，這時她叫住了他，對著他走過來，因為她知道他想保護她。

她牽起他的手。溫室那邊倚著一個梯子，因為他們已經準備整修溫室了，她打算說：「這需要五十英鎊。」不過她沒有說出口，而是改口提了賈斯柏獵鳥的事。

他說：「小男生就喜歡做這種事，他很快會找到更好的方法來娛樂自己。」

她的丈夫實在很明理。於是她說：「是的，孩子們都在經歷成長的階段。」她說完便凝視著花朵。

想法

• 這兩個人有向彼此坦露自己內心真實的想法嗎？
• 你能看得出來別人內心裡真正在想的事情嗎？

P.60

「你有聽過孩子們幫查爾斯‧湯司禮取的綽號嗎？」她問。「無神論者，他們稱他是小無神論者。祈求上帝不會讓他愛上菩露。」朗茲夫人說。

「如果她嫁給他，那就別想分到我的財產。」朗茲先生說。「雖然湯斯禮是個好好先生。」他補充道。

他們朝著劍葉蘭一路走去。「你在教你的女兒們誇大其辭。」朗茲先生責備她說。

「卡蜜拉阿姨比我嚴重多了。」朗茲夫人說。

「沒有人會把你的卡蜜拉阿姨當成模範。」朗茲先生說。

「她是我見過最美麗的女人了。」朗茲夫人說。

「天外有天，人外有人。」朗茲先生說。

「菩露以後會比我漂亮很多。」朗茲夫人說。

「我看不盡然。」朗茲先生說。

「我們欣賞一下今晚的夜色吧。」朗茲夫人說。

他們停下腳步。

「我希望安德魯要用功一點，不然會拿不到獎學金。」他說。

「噢，獎學金！」她說

「安德魯要是拿到獎學金，我會感到

很驕傲。」朗茲先生說。

「就算他沒拿到獎學金，我還是以他為榮。」她回答說。

P.61

他們在這一點上面，始終意見不一致，但這無傷大雅。她喜歡他對獎學金的重視，他也喜歡她不論安德魯做什麼，她都會感到驕傲。

這時，她突然想起斷崖那邊的小路。

「不是很晚了嗎？他們還沒回來。」她問。

他看看手錶。「現在才七點。」

他們來到了劍葉蘭旁的空地，在這裡又可以看到燈塔了，不過她並沒有望著燈塔。

這樣操心安德魯是沒有必要的，他在安德魯這個年紀時，常常一整天都在田野閒晃，那時也沒人會擔心他，或是害怕他會從斷崖上摔下去。

但她擔心的是男孩們，不是他。

他望著海灣，回憶起當年尚未成家之前，整天都在外面晃。那時走上一整天，都可能碰不到半個人。那邊的房子很少，方圓幾里內都沒有村子，可以想見那種情況。

他有時候會想起那邊唯一的一間小屋子——他停下來，嘆了口氣。他沒有那種權利了，他是八個孩子的父親——他提醒自己。「如果我想來個什麼改變，那我就是畜牲。」他想。「安德魯會成為一個比我更好的男人，苔露會像她媽媽說的那樣，變成一個大美女。要忙的事可多了——八個子女。」

P.62

他又嘆了口氣。

她聽到了便問：「你在嘆什麼氣？」

她猜他是在想——他要是沒有結婚的話，會寫出更好的作品。

「我不是在怨嘆什麼。」他說。

他牽起她的手，深深地親吻了一下。她的眼睛不禁濕濕了。他隨即把她的手放開。她知道他並不是在不滿什麼，他是沒有什麼事可抱怨的。

P.63

他們從眼前的景色中轉身離開，手挽著手，沿著小路走下去。「他生來就跟別人不一樣，」她想。「他對日常的事情又盲又聾又啞，但對形而上的東西卻異常的敏銳。他有注意到那些花嗎？沒有！他有留意到眼前的景色嗎？沒有！他會不會連餐盤或烤牛肉上面是不是放了布甸都不清楚？他跟大家一起坐在餐桌上時，其實像是在夢遊的狀態裡。」

就在此時，他說「很漂亮」。這其實

只是為了討好她。他假裝他很欣賞那些花，但她知道其實不然，他甚至連旁邊有沒有花也不會注意到。他會這樣說，純粹是為了討好她。

他們看到前方的小路上有兩個人。「啊，那不是莉莉・布斯克在和威廉・班克斯在散步嗎？」她想。「對，沒錯。這是不是就表示他們兩個人會結婚？對，就是這樣！這太好了！他們兩個人一定要結婚！」

莉莉・布斯克和威廉・班克斯這時正在聊著藝術，有很多繪畫莉莉都還沒親眼目睹過。「也許不要看太多畫比較好，」她說：「那樣只會讓我對自己的作品更加不滿意而已。」

P.64

班克斯先生說：「我們無法每一個人都變成大師或是達爾文，但如果沒有像我們這樣的凡夫俗子，又如何能烘托出達爾文或大師嗎？」

莉莉想恭維他一下，便說：「班克斯先生，您就不是一個平凡的人。」

但他要的不是恭維（莉莉以為大部分人都喜歡）。當他們走到草地的盡頭時，他們轉過身，瞧見了朗茲夫婦。

「婚姻就這麼一回事，」莉莉想，「一個男人，一個女人，看著一個女孩在丟球。」

他們夫妻緊緊相依地站著，看著菩露和賈斯柏玩接球和丟球。這一刻，他們成了婚姻的化身：丈夫與妻子。

朗茲夫人向他們笑了笑打招呼（噢，她一定是在想我們要結婚了，莉莉猜想），然後說：「班克斯先生說好了今天晚上要和我們一起用晚餐。」

球飛得很高，他們盯著球，球不見了，他們看到了一顆星星。

菩露跑過去撿球，她的母親說：「他們回來了嗎？南西有跟他們一起回來嗎？」

南西和他們一起出門，是蜜塔・朵伊找她一起去的。她雖然不是很想去，但還是跟去了。

P.65

他們到了海邊後，便各自帶開。安德魯去找螃蟹，留下他們兩個人。南西坐在潮水潭的岩石邊，也留下他們兩個人。她將水坑變成大海，將小魚變成鯊魚和鯨魚。她用手擋住陽光，在她圍出的小小世界裡投下大大的雲影。她像上帝那樣，為無數的無辜生靈帶來黑暗與淒涼。接著她又很快把手移開，讓陽光灑落下來。

「海浪來了。」安德魯喊道。

南西於是向海邊跑去，在那裡的一塊岩石後方——哦，天啊，保羅和蜜塔，

他們互相擁抱著，大概是在親吻吧。她看了很生氣。她和安德魯不發一語地各自穿上襪子和鞋子，沒有對這件事情說什麼。

P.66

「對，」菩露回答母親說：「我想南西有跟他們一起去。」

那麼南西就是跟他們一起出門了，朗茲夫人想。房門傳來了敲門聲，朗茲夫人放下梳子，說：「請進！」

進來的是賈斯柏和蘿絲。南西跟他們在一起，比較不會出事情，還是比較會出事情？朗茲夫人判斷，應該比較不會出事情吧。他們不可能全部都被海浪捲走。

「蘿絲，我應該戴哪一條珠寶項鍊比較好？」她問。

賈斯柏挑了一條蛋白石項鍊給她，蘿絲挑的是金項鍊。哪一條和黑色禮服比較搭？

「親愛的，選一條吧。」她說。

她讓他們慢慢挑。她讓蘿絲仔細瞧這條項鍊，然後拿項鍊對著黑色禮服比了比。她知道蘿絲很喜歡這種挑選珠寶的小小盛典，他們每晚都會進行一次。

這時，他們聽到銅鑼的洪大聲音，這是用來通知各處的人，不管是在閣樓、在臥室，是在看書、在寫東西或是在梳頭髮，請大家立即停下手邊的事，前往飯廳用餐。

「我現在準備好要下樓吃飯囉。」朗茲夫人說。

P.68

「我對自己的人生做了什麼？」朗茲夫人坐在餐桌的首位上，心裡頭想著這個問題。「威廉，你坐在我旁邊，」她說，「莉莉，」她疲倦地說：「坐那邊。」

猶如烏雲籠罩一般，所有的東西瞬間失去色彩。這個房間（她環顧一下）很陳舊了，四處都看不到任何美麗的東西。她很快地抖擻起精神，就像甩甩停擺的手錶一樣。接著，她轉向威廉‧班克斯，可憐的男人！他沒有妻兒，子然一人地吃著飯。她同情起他，於是開始打開話匣子。

「你找到你的信了嗎？蜜德莉幫你把信放在廳廊那邊。」她對威廉‧班克斯說道。

莉莉‧布斯克看著她。「她看起來好蒼老。」莉莉想。「她幹嘛要同情威廉‧班克斯？她搞錯了。他並不可憐，他有自己的事業，」莉莉自言自語道。她也有她自己的工作。

這時，她看到了自己的畫，她想：

「對了，我要把樹畫在中間。我接下來就要來畫樹，這就是我一直難以下筆的地方。」

她拿起鹽巴罐，然後把它擱在有花卉圖樣的餐桌布上，好提醒自己要把樹移開。

「郵箱裡通常不會有什麼重要的東西，但很奇怪的是，人還是會想要收到信。」班克斯先生說。

「他們在扯什麼廢話啊。」查爾斯‧湯司禮心想。

P.69

「您常寫信嗎，湯司禮先生？」朗茲夫人問。

她也同情他，莉莉心想。

「我會寫信給我母親。」湯司禮先生回答。他並不打算聊這些愚蠢婦女所聊的這種無意義話題。

他上一刻還在自己的房間裡看書，而這一刻卻顯得這麼愚蠢。她們幹嘛為了晚餐盛裝打扮？他就穿著他最普通的衣服下樓。她們無所事事，只會聊天吃飯，這是女性的通病，她們的愚蠢無法誕生出文明。

「朗茲夫人，我們明天是去不了燈塔了。」他說。

他喜歡她，景仰她，但他覺得有必要提這件事。

「他真是她所見過最無趣的男人了。」莉莉‧布斯克心想。既然如此，她又何必把他的話放在心上？「女人不會畫畫，女人不會寫作。」

「噢，湯司禮先生，帶我和您一起去看燈塔吧，我很想去。」她說。

他知道她說的不是真話。她是在嘲笑他。他覺得很孤單。她才不想跟他一起去看燈塔，她鄙視他，菩露‧朗茲也是，她們所有人都是。不過，他是不會被女性愚弄的，於是他轉過頭，望著窗外，然後很失禮地說道：「明天對你來說風太了，你會生病的。」

P.70

接著，他轉過頭要對朗茲夫人說話，不過朗茲夫人這時正在和威廉‧班克斯講話。

「但願我沒有來這裡，我可以好好工作。」班克斯先生想。

「你一定很討厭這樣吵吵鬧鬧的晚餐吧。」朗茲夫人說。

班克斯先生回答：「不，一點也不會。」

「他在說假話。」湯司禮先生心想，「朗茲夫婦言不及義。」他想。要跟他們這次一起度假還可以，但下次就免了。女人很無聊。當然，茲朗沒有退路了，他娶了一個嬌妻，生了八個孩子。

「一定是他們回來了。」朗茲夫人望著門心想。

就在這時，蜜塔‧朵伊、保羅‧瑞雷和捧著一大盤菜的女僕一起走進門。

「我們太晚了。」蜜塔說道。他們各自走向餐桌的不同方位。

「我的別針掉了，那是我祖母留下來的別針。」蜜塔難過地說。她在朗茲先生的旁邊坐了下來，棕色的大眼睛流露著憂傷的神情。

「你怎麼會這麼笨，戴著珠寶去爬岩石？」他問。

131

P.71

朗茲夫人心想,「那他們一定是求婚、許下終身了。保羅要坐在我旁邊,我為他留了座位。」

「我們回去找蜜塔的別針。」他在朗茲夫人的旁邊坐下時說道。

「我們」——這就足夠說明了,她知道這是他第一次用了「我們」這個字眼。我們做了這個,我們做了那個,「他們這一輩子會不斷地這樣說。」她想。

就在這時,女僕打開盤蓋,一大盤褐色的食物送出了香噴噴的橄欖味。這道菜廚子在三天前就開始準備了。

「真好吃!」班克斯先生說。

「這是我祖母傳下來的法國料理配方。」朗茲夫人說。

「蜜塔是在哪裡掉了別針的?」莉莉問。

「在海邊,我明天會再去找找看。」保羅說。

莉莉穿著一件灰色的小洋裝,搭配她蒼白的臉色和中國式的小眼睛,她的光芒被蜜塔蓋了過去。

「她的什麼都好小,」朗茲夫人在心裡把兩人做比較,「不過,等莉莉到了四十歲時,她的狀況看起來會比蜜塔好。莉莉的一些特質我很喜歡,不過我想男人大概不懂得欣賞,除非是有一點年紀的男人,像威廉·班克斯這樣。威廉會娶莉莉,他們兩個人有好多共通點,他們都喜歡花卉,而且個性比較冷淡,不是那麼友善。我應該幫他們安排一下,讓他們可以一起散步得久一點。」我真笨,把兩個人安排坐在彼此的對

面。「我明天要把位置安排好,明天如果放晴,我們就會去野餐。」她想。每一件事情看起來都有可能發生,而且好像都很妥當。

P.73

她放下湯匙,聽他丈夫發言。他正在講一千兩百五十三的開根號,這到底是在說什麼?她到現在還是搞不懂。開根號?那是什麼?兒子們才懂。立方,根號,他們現在在聊這個。男人真是聰明呀。之後,威廉·班克斯稱讚起「威弗萊」系列小說。

「你想這系列小說能夠紅多久?」有人問道。

朗茲夫人嗅到了這個問題對丈夫可能會引爆的危險。她想:「這種問題會讓他想到自己的作品反應不佳。他會想:『我的書能夠被青睞多久?』」

威廉·班克斯笑了笑(他對名氣是不屑一顧的),說道:「風潮怎麼改變並不重要。在文學或是任何領域上,又有

誰能夠預測潮流的消長？我們應該把握眼前的才是。」他說。

朗茲夫人知道朗茲先生開始覺得不自在了。他希望聽到有人說「喔，朗茲先生，像您的作品會流傳很久」之類的話。

他說司各特（還是莎士比亞？）的作品，他終身都會閱讀，他動了怒氣地說。她想，大家聽到他這樣講，應該都會覺得有點怪怪的吧。

蜜塔‧朵伊接著說：「我不認為有誰是真的喜歡讀莎士比亞的作品。」

P.74

朗茲先生說：「只有很少的人真的如他們所說的那樣喜歡莎士比亞的作品。」他又補了一句，「不過他的有些劇本是寫得很精彩。」

朗茲夫人覺得此時此刻的氣氛才是正常的。「他會揶揄一下蜜塔，而蜜塔會用某種方式來讚美他。」

這時，她看了一下子女們。菩露一直好奇地盯著蜜塔看。朗茲夫人心想，「你以後也會和這幾天的蜜塔一樣地幸福。」她補充道：「你會比她更幸福，因為你是我的女兒。」她的女兒一定要比別人家的女兒幸福才行。

最後，晚餐結束，大家都離開了餐廳。朗茲夫人在走廊上站了一會兒，望著窗外。窗外正刮著風。

P.75

「他們一輩子都不會忘記今天這個夜晚，不會忘記這樣的月亮，這樣的風，這個房子，還有我。」她想著，內心不禁感到滿足。「終其他們的一生，我在他們的心裡都留下了一個位置。」

她微笑著，走進另一個房間，她的丈夫正坐在裡頭看書。

她看著丈夫（當她拾起襪子開始編織時），看到他一副不想被打擾的樣子。他正讀得入迷，她看到那是沃爾特‧司各特爵士的小說。

查爾斯‧湯司禮剛剛說人們不再讀司各特的小說了，這讓她丈夫聯想到：「人們也會這樣說我。」於是他就去拿了司各特的書來看。他一直很在意自己的作品——人們會讀他的書嗎？他的書夠好嗎？人們又是如何看待他的？

她繼續一邊編織、一邊心想著。接著，她看了丈夫一眼，他們的眼神交會了一下，但彼此並不想交談。不要打斷我看書，這大概就是他要講的話。什麼話都不要說，坐在那裡就好。他繼續看著他的書。這本書很吸引人，他沉浸其中，覺得意興風發，今天晚上那些不愉快的瑣事全被拋到腦後。他一邊讀著書

（這是沃爾特‧司各特爵士最好的作品），一邊任自己的眼淚滑下，他把自己的各種煩惱和失敗都拋到九霄雲外了。

P.76

「就任他們去改善吧。」他看完一個章節後說道。他們是無法改善的。如果年輕人不重視這本書，那他們當然也就不會看重他的作品。他看看妻子，她也正看著書，她看書的表情很平靜。他喜歡和她單獨坐在一起。

朗茲夫人這時注意到丈夫正在盯著她看。他對她笑了笑，心裡想著：「你繼續看你的書吧。你現在看起來不悲傷了。」

他想知道她在看什麼書。他喜歡把她看成是一個不夠聰明、沒有學識的人。他懷疑她是否真能讀懂書上所寫的內容。可能不是很懂，他想。她長得真是漂亮。

「怎樣呢？」她放下書本，說道：「他們互許終身了，」她一邊說，一邊開始編織，「保羅和蜜塔。」

「我也是這樣想。」他說。

這件事也沒什麼可以多說的。她還在想著剛剛讀到詩，而他在看完他的書之後，思緒也還沉浸在當中。於是他們都只靜靜地坐著。

P.77

他還在盯著她看，不過他的神情改變了。他希望她能跟他說她愛他，但是她說不出這樣的話。他覺得說話沒那麼難，但她卻覺得很難。他可以把事情說出來，而她卻做不到。他說她是一個冷感的女人。

她站起來，立在窗邊，手裡拿著棕色的襪子。她一方面想避開他，另一方面也是因為她想到海邊的夜色通常都很美。她知道他正看著她，也知道他在想什麼，「你比以前更美了。」

她覺得夜色好美。

「你不跟我說你愛我嗎？」

她就是說不出口。

她沒有開口說話，而是轉過身來看著他。她看到他時，便笑了起來。

他知道她是愛他的，這一點不容懷疑。

她又望向窗外笑了笑，對自己說：「塵世上的一切都比不上此刻的幸福。」

II. 歲月流逝

P.78

黑夜如今變得風嘯呼呼，一片淒涼。樹木被吹得東倒西歪，樹葉倉皇飛落，鋪滿了草地，塞滿了排水溝，把排水管堵塞住，小路上也撒落了滿地。

在一個天色尚暗的清晨裡，朗茲先生伸出雙臂，腳步蹣跚地踽踽獨行著。朗茲夫人在昨晚突然撒手人寰。他的雙手什麼也沒抓到。

這個房子已經人去樓空，門都上了鎖，窗簾飛舞著，木頭嘎嘎作響，鍋盤瓷器都破損了。

轉眼已經春天，菩露‧朗茲出閣了。大家都說她看起來好美啊！

然而，很不幸地，就在那一年的夏天，菩露‧朗茲因為分娩而染病去世了。

人們說這真是一個悲劇，原本應該是要有一個幸福的未來才對。

P.80

那個夏末，傳來了不祥的聲音，聽起來宛若敲鋤頭的聲音。碗櫥裡不時傳來玻璃的鏗鏘聲，彷彿有一個極其痛苦的巨大叫喊聲震晃了玻璃。接著再度寧靜下來。之後，夜復一夜，有時是在正中午，會傳來東西掉落的重擊聲。

有一顆砲彈爆炸了。在法國，有二、三十個年輕人被炸死，其中包括了安德魯·朗茲。謝天謝地，他是瞬間死亡的。海面上現在被染上了一塊紫色，看起來像是在不可見的深海下，有東西在沸騰著，汩汩流著血。

P.81

光陰

・歲月流逝，朗茲家發生了哪些事？

☐朗茲夫人：去世了

☐菩露：去世了

☐安德魯：去世了

P.82

那個春天，卡邁可先生出版了一本詩集，結果銷售很好。人們說，戰爭讓重新喚回了人們對詩的興趣。

「這家人不會重返故居了。房子在秋天時大概就會拍賣掉。」人們說。

臥室的衣櫃裡還放著衣服，「這些衣服應該怎麼處理？」麥納夫人心想，「朗茲夫人的東西也都還在，這位可憐的女士！這些東西她再也用不到了。他們說她走了，幾年前在倫敦時過世了。」那裡有一件她做園藝時會穿的灰色舊斗篷（麥納夫人看過她穿過）。

P.83

她能看得到她，她那時帶著清洗的衣物，從車道那邊走過來，一路欣賞著花朵。屋子裡還有靴子和鞋子，化妝檯上面還放著一把梳子和髮梳。「看起來就好像她明天就會回來了一樣。」她想。（聽說她走得很突然。）

因為戰爭的關係，他們已經有好幾年沒回來過這裡。很多事情都已經人事已非，有很多家庭失去了親人。朗茲夫人走了，安德魯先生殉難了，菩露小姐也過世了，聽說她初胎的這個寶寶也難產了。在大戰期間，每個人都有喪慟。

後來，一位年輕的小姐突然寫信給麥納夫人，請她把房子打掃一下，他們大概會在夏天時過來。房子裡的擺設都沒有被動過，他們希望保持原樣。

麥納夫人拿來了掃帚和水桶，她刷刷洗洗，緩慢而費力地打掃，讓房子暫緩了毀壞。她從「歲月池」裡救回了一個櫥櫃、一塊地毯、一個茶杯組和書本。在幾天的賣力打掃之後，房子終於可以住人了。

九月的這個傍晚，莉莉·布斯克帶著行李來到了屋子前面。古邁可先生也搭了同一班火車過來。

黑夜的帷幕裹住自己，也籠罩了房子，籠罩了古邁可先生和莉莉·布斯克。島嶼四周的海浪嘆息聲，撫慰了他們的心靈。沒有東西打擾他們的夜夢，直到陽光掀開了帷幕。莉莉·布斯克睜開雙眼，她重回這個地方了，她坐在床上，想著。

III. 燈塔

P. 84

經過了這麼多年，在朗茲夫人過世之後重返舊地，她是什麼樣的感受？莉莉·布斯克自問著。沒有，沒什麼感受。她昨天深夜才抵達這裡，一切都是那麼神祕、黑暗。她現在獨自坐在早餐的餐桌旁，現在時候還早，還沒到八點。

朗茲先生、卡梅和詹姆士準備去燈塔，他們應該要上路了——他們得趕漲落潮還是什麼的。但卡梅還沒準備好、詹姆士也還沒準備好，南西忘了訂三明治，朗茲先生已經等得不耐煩了，他重重地關上門走出去。

「現在去那裡有什麼用？」他氣呼呼地說。

她獨自坐在擺放著乾淨茶杯的長桌子旁。這個房子，這個地方，這個早晨，這一切都讓她感到陌生。她對這裡並沒有感情。

「感覺很不真實。」她一邊想，一邊盯著自己的空咖啡杯，「朗茲夫人走了，安德魯走了，菩露也走了。」而她並沒有什麼特別的感覺。

這時，從窗邊走過的朗茲先生突然抬起頭，張大眼睛，直直地猛盯著她看。莉莉假裝在喝她的空咖啡杯，不想跟他講話。

P. 85

他對她搖了搖頭，然後繼續往前走去。（她聽到他說：「孤伶伶地。」聽到他說：「死去。」）他想要一點關愛，但莉莉並不想理會他。

這時，她突然想起來，自己十年前坐在這個位置上時，桌布上有一個小小的葉子圖樣。那時她的畫遇到瓶頸，她當時說要把樹移到中間，而那幅畫到現在都還沒有完成。「我現在要來把它完成。」她想。「我的畫在哪裡？」她納悶著。「最後那個晚上，我把畫放在大廳裡。我要立刻動工。」

她趁著朗茲先生還沒繞回來之前，很快地站起來。

她把畫架架在草地上。「對，我十年前就是站在這裡，那邊有牆，有樹籬，有樹木。」她想。這些年來，這幅畫面一直留在她的腦海裡，現在她可以把它完成了。

莉莉的繪畫

- 請翻回第 49 頁。是誰在對莉莉的繪畫下評語？
- 她為什麼不把畫完成？

P. 87

莉莉在畫架上鋪上乾淨的畫布。她用力地盯著畫布看，但就是沒有畫面浮現出來。

「那些孩子什麼時候會過來？他們什麼時候要去燈塔？」她希望朗茲先生也會去。朗茲先生不懂得付出，她想這一點就生氣。他只接受，都是朗茲夫人在付出的。她付出，不斷地付出，如今她已經走了。這都是朗茲夫人的過失。她走了。這回是今年四十四歲的莉莉，她站在那裡玩畫畫，虛擲光陰。這都是朗茲夫人的錯。她走了。她以前常坐的台階空無人影。她人已經走了。

「他們不應該找我來的。我不應該來的。」她想。

詹姆士和卡梅來到露台上，嚴肅而憂傷的兩個人。朗茲先生的肩膀上背了一個帆布背包。之後他開路前進，孩子們跟在後面。

莉莉站在那裡看著他們離去，心想：「那是何等的一張臉！是什麼造就了這樣的一張臉？」她猜想。「夜夜的思索，思索廚房桌子的實體。」她記的這個比喻，那是安德魯跟她說的。（他遭遇爆炸，當場死亡，她這才想起。）

「不會畫，不會寫。」她喃喃自語道。查爾斯·湯司禮老愛這樣說，她記得。

P. 88

接著她想起海灘上的那一幕。那是一個吹著風的早上，大夥兒都來到了海邊。朗茲夫人坐在岩石邊寫信，一封信、一封信地寫著。查爾斯·湯司禮大獻殷

勤，和莉莉玩著遊戲。他們一起揀黑色的扁平小石頭，然後對著海面打水漂兒。

朗茲夫人不時地抬起頭，對著他們笑。她記得他們那時候玩得很愉快，而朗茲夫人就在一旁看著他們。朗茲夫人讓海灘上的這一幕留了下來，讓這個時刻成了友情和喜好的一刻。經過這麼多年之後，仍然歷歷在目，就像一幅繪畫作品一般。

她要休息一下。休息之際，亙古的問題又浮現了。生命的意義是什麼？這個簡單的問題，卻始終找不到答案。大概永遠都不會有答案。有的只是生活中的小小奇蹟，像是黑暗中閃現的柴火。這一幕就是。她自己，查爾斯・湯司禮，大海，朗茲夫人把這三者結合成了畫面，是她讓那一刻剎那成永恆的。

「生命佇足在這裡。」朗茲夫人說。

「朗茲夫人！朗茲夫人！」她重覆喊道。

莉莉把身子往後退，看著自己的畫。她蘸了蘸藍色顏料，自己也沉浸在過去裡。

P.90

朗茲夫人這時站起身來，她記得。差不多要走回去了，午餐時間快到了。大夥兒於是一起離開海灘。她和威廉・班克斯走在後頭，保羅和蜜塔走在他們前面。

「瑞雷夫婦，」莉莉・布斯克一邊擠出綠色顏料，一邊想到，「他們的婚姻後來很不好。他們在婚後的第一年之後，婚姻就開始出現問題。兩個人已經不再『相愛』。保羅在外面有了女人，那是一個個性嚴肅的女人。她去參加集會，他們兩個人對事情有相同的看法。」

「這就是瑞雷夫婦的故事。」莉莉想。她想像自己正在跟朗茲夫人講這件事。她會很好奇瑞雷夫婦後來的情況。莉莉會很高興跟朗茲夫人分享一場失敗的婚姻。

她會跟她說：「事情的發展和你所希望的都不一樣，他們的幸福是那樣的，我的幸福是這樣的。一切都人事已非了。」這一刻，朗茲夫人被塵封了，她只屬於過去。這一刻，莉莉覺得自己贏了朗茲夫人。「她一定想不到保羅在外面會有女人。她不會知道我站在這裡畫畫，始終單身，並沒有嫁給威廉・班克斯。」

朗茲夫人想湊合他們，如果她還活著，他們大概真的就結婚了。在那個夏天，他是「最好心的男士」，他是「一時之選的科學家，我丈夫說。」他也是「可憐的威廉——我去他家時，看了很難過，他的屋子裡什麼都沒有，也沒有人來插花。」

P.91

所以啦，她要他們一起去散步。「她怎麼會對婚姻那麼狂熱？」莉莉看著自己的畫，心裡很納悶。「她好險逃過一劫。」她想。她看著桌布，想到自己應該要把樹木移到中間。她才不需要結婚，她感到一陣強烈的喜悅，「現在我可以大無畏地面對朗茲夫人了。」她想。

事實上，她和威廉·班克斯的友誼，是她生命中一個喜悅的源泉。她愛威廉·班克斯。

卡邁可先生躺在椅子上，兩手攔在肚子上。他的書掉落在草地上了。

「這一切，有何意義？」她想問卡邁可先生，但她沒問。

她看著自己的畫。那就是他的答案吧，她想。諸行無常，萬物都在變化之中，除了文字、除了繪畫。畫面被留了下來。

淚水在她的眼裡打轉，從臉頰上滑落了下來。她為朗茲夫人而哭泣。

她又看了看卡邁可老先生。這一刻她感覺到，如果此時他們都站起身來，要求一個答案：「生命為何如此短暫？如此難解？」這樣空間就會被填起來，現出人形，如果他們叫得夠大聲，朗茲夫人就會回來。

「朗茲夫人！」她大聲喊道：「朗茲夫人！」她的臉上淌落滾滾淚水。

P.92

那查爾斯·湯司禮現在怎樣了呢？她想知道。他拿到了研究員的職位，也結了婚。他現在住在果戈林區。在戰爭期間，她有一次在一個大廳裡聽到他在發言。他當時在公開指控一些事情：他在譴責某個人。

艷陽高照，船隻這時突然停下來，離燈塔還有幾哩遠。

朗茲先生正在看著書。在父親閱讀之際，詹姆士生怕他會抬起頭來，問道：「我們為什麼會坐在這裡？」

「如果他真這樣問了，」詹姆士心想，「那我會拿起刀子，朝他的心臟刺穿過去。」

他心裡頭一直有著這個古老的象徵畫面：拿刀刺穿父親的心臟。只是現在他想著：「這個老人並不是我真正想殺的人，我只是想起來對抗，擺脫欺凌。」他記得父親說：「會下雨，你們是去不了燈塔的。」

船帆一陣晃動，船身又動了起來，乘風破浪迅速前進。朗茲先生坐在那裡，海風吹得他的髮絲飛揚。

「他看起來很老了。」詹姆士心想。

「我餓了。」朗茲先生一邊說，一邊冷不防地闔上書本。「午餐時間到了。還有，你們看！」他說。「燈塔在那裡，我們快到了。」

P.94

「他船駕得很好，」老船夫馬卡稱讚詹姆士說：「駕得真穩。」

而他父親，從來不曾稱讚過他，詹姆士心懷不滿。

她望著石階，空無人影。她看著畫，之後在中間畫上一條線。完成了，畫完成了。

她疲憊地擱下畫筆，心想：「這樣就對了，我已經畫出我所見的了。」

P. 95

莉莉的所見

・莉莉的所見是什麼？
　□一個有房子、草坪、大海和
　　燈塔的畫面
　□一個表現生命意義的畫面
　□一個母與子的畫面
　□一個永恆的剎那

朗茲先生打開包裹，拿出三明治分給大家吃。接著，他得意洋洋地說：「詹姆士，你太厲害了！你駕起船來跟真正的船夫沒兩樣。」

「就是這個了！」卡梅心想，她小聲地對詹姆士說：「你終於聽到了。」她知道這正是詹姆士想要的。父親已經開口稱讚過他了。

這時，他們已經能看到燈塔上的那兩個人，他們正望著他們，準備接風。

朗茲先生戴上帽子。「那些包裹要帶上去。」他說。

「他應該已經抵達燈塔了。」莉莉・布斯可說罷，便覺得一陣疲憊。

「他上岸了，」她說，「完成了。」

她很快轉過頭面向畫作，這就是她的畫，一片藍藍綠綠。「就掛在閣樓吧，」她想，「那又有何妨？」

ANSWER KEY

Before Reading

Page 8

2 calm

Page 9

5 (possible answers)

a) Mr Ramsay, because he didn't pursue his studies to the full.
b) Facing life and daily events in a heroic way.
c) Mrs Ramsay

Page 10

6 a) 2   b) 1   c) 4   d) 3

Page 11

7
a) dull   b) talented   c) disagreeable
d) bad-tempered   e) independent
f) scruffy

Page 12

8
a) stupidity   b) failure   c) admired
d) uncharming   e) confided

Page 13

9 a) 2   b) 2

Page 28

• Mrs Ramsay and Lily are in the garden.
• Lily is painting Mrs Ramsay's portrait.
• Mr Ramsay runs across the lawn shouting.

Page 45

• Charles Tansley, Augustus Carmichael, Lily Briscoe, William Bankes

Page 59

No.

Page 81

• Mrs Ramsay has died. Prue has died. Andrew has died.

Page 85

• William Bankes.
• Because the painting had puzzled her. She had wanted to move the tree to the middle of the picture but then never finished it.

Page 95 (possible answers)

• A vision of the meaning of life
• A vision of mother and child
• A vision of a moment in time

After Reading

Page 97

1
a) Mrs Ramsay   b) Mr Tansley
c) Miss Briscoe   d) Mr Bankes
e) Mr Tansley   f) Mrs Ramsay

4 (possible answers)
• Literature and Art: b, d, e
• Women and Marriage: a, b, c, f

Page 98

5 a) F   b) F   c) T   d) F   e) T   f) F

6

a) They have eight children.
b) She doesn't have a career.
c) True, but she does let William Bankes have a look.

d) They tease Charles Tansley.

f) They are for the Lighthouse keeper's little boy.

7

a) coat   b) brooch   c) slippers
d) penknife   e) red-hot pokers   f) cloak

Page 99

8

a) 7   b) 3   c) 6   d) 1   e) 2   f) 4   g) 5

9

a) Mrs Ramsay   b) Miss Briscoe
c) Mr Tansley   d) Miss Briscoe
e) Mr Ramsay   f) Mr Ramsay
g) Mr Tansley

Page 100

11 Lily Briscoe

12 (possible answers)
• Like: dynamic, intelligent
• Don't like: bad-tempered, self-centered, selfish

13 (possible answers)
• Like: unselfish, kind, dutiful, generous, modest
• Don't like: domineering, arrogant

15

a) Mr Bankes   b) Mr Ramsay
c) Mr Tansley   d) Mr Ramsay
e) Mr Carmichael   f) Mr Tansley
g) Mr Bankes   h) Mr Carmichael
i) Mr Bankes

Page 102

16

a) 2   b) 5   c) 1   d) 3   e) 4

Page 103

18 a) T   b) F   c) T   d) T   e) T   f) T

19

a) 51   b) one day   c) 4
d) 10 years   e) 8   f) a morning
g) The passing of time is not important; a moment in time is more important

Page 104

21

a) had died   b) had had an affair
c) had died   d) had died
e) had got his fellowship and had married
f) had brought out a book of poems

22 (possible answers)

a) People should marry.
b) Children should be aware that life is difficult.
c) Lily Briscoe should fall in love with Mr Tansley. / Lily Briscoe should marry.
d) Mrs Ramsay shouldn't interfere in other people's lives. / Mrs Ramsay should know that Mr Ramsay was much more important than she was.
e) Prue shouldn't fall in love with Mr Tansley. / Prue should never have married.
f) Mr Ramsay should never have married.
g) James and Cam should fight tyranny to the death.

Page 105

23

a) death   b) teeth   c) bullying
d) temper   e) date   f) boats

24

a) the Lighthouse keeper   b) Lily Briscoe
c) James   d) Mr Ramsay
e) Mrs Ramsay   f) Mr Ramsay

Test

1

a) 2   b) 2   c) 3   d) 1   e) 3   f) 2

2

a) 4   b) 6   c) 7   d) 5   e) 2

f) 3   g) 9   h) 1   i) 8

國家圖書館出版品預行編目資料

燈塔行 / Elspeth Rawstron 著；安卡斯譯. 一初版.
一[臺北市] : 寂天文化, 2012.12
面；公分.

中英對照

ISBN 978-986-318-051-7 (25K平裝附光碟片)

1.英語 2.讀本

805.18   101021658

原著 _ Virginia Woolf
改寫 _ Elspeth Rawstron
譯者 _ 安卡斯
校對 _ 陳慧莉
封面設計 _ 蔡怡柔
主編 _ 黃鈺云
製程管理 _ 蔡智堯
出版者 _ 寂天文化事業股份有限公司
電話 _ +886-2-2365-9739
傳真 _ +886-2-2365-9835
網址 _ www.icosmos.com.tw
讀者服務 _ onlineservice@icosmos.com.tw
出版日期 _ 2012年12月 初版一刷（250101）
郵撥帳號 _ 1998620-0 寂天文化事業股份有限公司
訂購金額600 （含）元以上郵資免費
訂購金額600元以下者，請外加郵資60元
若有破損，請寄回更換

〔限台灣銷售〕